LAST LOVE
IN
CONSTANTINOPLE

By the same author

Dictionary of the Khazars
Landscape Painted with Tea
The Inner Side of the Wind

Milorad Pavić

LAST LOVE IN CONSTANTINOPLE

A Tarot novel for divination

Translated from the Serbian by
Christina Pribichevich-Zorić

PETER OWEN
LONDON AND CHESTER SPRINGS

PETER OWEN PUBLISHERS
73 Kenway Road, London SW5 ORE
Peter Owen books are distributed in the USA by Dufour Editions Inc.,
Chester Springs, PA 19425-0007

First published in Great Britain 1998
© Milorad Pavić 1994
English translation © Christina Pribichevich-Zorić 1998
Illustrations © Ivan Pavić

ISBN 0 7206 1035 4

A catalogue record for this book is available from the British Library

Printed and made in Great Britain by Hillman Printers (Frome) Ltd.

The Major Arcana (Great Secret) is the name of a deck of twenty-two cards used for divination. These cards are marked by numbers 0 to 21 and, together with the other, larger deck of fifty-six cards (the Minor Arcana), they comprise the Tarot (Tarroc, Tarocchi). The origin of the Tarot is associated with the priests (Hierophants) of the Eleusinian Mysteries in Greece, and some believe that the Tarot stems from the tradition of the cults of Hermes. The cards are often used for fortune-telling by gypsies who are believed to have brought this secret 'language' from Chaldea and Egypt to Israel and Greece, with it later spreading along the shores of the Mediterranean. As far as is known, the Tarot has been in circulation for about seven centuries in Central Europe, France and Italy and is today a universally known game. The oldest preserved examples of Tarot cards date from 1390 and 1445 (the Minchiati set from the Museo Correr in Venice).

The Major Arcana is usually divided into three groups of seven cards each. In divination, the meaning of each card individually and in relation to the others is interpreted by the reader, who knows the established meanings (keys) of the cards, or who ascribes them a meaning which he keeps secret. The meaning of the Tarot card changes depending on whether the card is laid out right side up or upside down, because in the case of the latter it means the opposite of the card's basic meaning. Today the Tarot and its keys are the subject of countless, often very different handbooks. At the root of the Tarot lies the symbolic language of the collective mind of man. The symbols and keys of the Tarot are aimed at ancient Greece, at the Caballa, at astrology, numerology and so on. Mystic energy and esoteric wisdom are attained through twenty-one initiations by the Fool – the symbol of the card that is simultaneously the zero, the middle and the last card of the Tarot's 'Great Secret'.

To Use the Book for Divination

You may read the novel in sequence. Alternatively, you may choose to lay the cards out in one of the three patterns described in Appendix 1 (the Magic Cross, the Great Triad or the Celtic Cross) and read the corresponding chapters in the sequence suggested by the Tarot. This method allows the possibility of divination or fortune-telling by means of the cards.

If you wish to read your own fortune, take the deck of Tarot cards, shuffle and cut them. Make a note of the card numbers in the order they appear after shuffling. Fan the cards out face down so that you may choose the cards you wish to lay out. If you choose to lay them out according to the Magic Cross, pick five cards and lay them out in the shape of the Magic Cross. The sequence in which they are to be turned over is given in Appendix 1. An interpretation of each card may be found at the end of the book in Appendix 2. The corresponding book chapter further explains the card. You can read this yourself or have it read to you. Then move on to the next card.

If you wish someone else to read the cards for you, take the Tarot deck and let the Reader shuffle the cards; then you must cut the deck with your left hand. The Reader will then make a note of the cards as they were shuffled and fan them out face down on the table. You will pick your cards and toss them on the table, following the layout chosen by the Reader. The Reader will then lay out the cards and interpret them for you.

Contents

The Keys of the Great Secret
For Ladies of Both Sexes

ᒉHE ᒉOOL

ᒉN addition to his mother tongue, he also spoke Greek, French, Italian and Turkish. He was born in Trieste into a family of Serbian merchants and patrons of the theatre, who had ships in the Adriatic and wheat and vineyards on the Danube. Since childhood he had served in the unit of his father, French cavalry officer Haralampije Opujić. He knew that when charging on horseback or making love exhaling was more important than inhaling. He wore the splendid robes of a cavalryman. In the middle of winter he slept in the snow underneath the covered wagon rather than evict from it his Russian hound bitch and her litter, and in the middle of war he wept over his ruined yellow cavalier boots; he left service in the infantry in order not to part from his cavalry gear. He was mad about beautiful horses and plaited their tails. He obtained his silver tableware in Vienna, adored fancy dress balls, masquerades and fireworks and felt like a fish in water when in drawing rooms and inns graced by women and music.

His father used to say of him that he was as foolish as the first wind and was treading on the edge of a precipice. One minute he looked like his mother, the next like his grandfather and the next like his still unborn son or granddaughter. He was a most hand-some man, taller than average, with a pale face, a dim-ple like a navel in his chin and his long, thick hair as black as coal. He sported his finely twirled eyebrows like a moustache, and his moustache braided like a whip. On his endless military expeditions in Bavaria, Silesia and Italy women admired his appearance, his horsemanship and long, combed hair which, when he was tired of marches and the hardships of military life, he would dry by the hearth in a wayside inn; for fun they would dress him in women's clothes, stick a white rose in his hair, take his last penny at the tavern dance, give him their beds when he was ill or tired and tear-fully part with the cavalry units at the end of their win-ter respite. But he, he was wont to say that all his memories were in his food bag.

With an alien feminine smile on his face and his growth of beard, young Opujić had crossed Europe, first as a boy with his father and later on his own in the French cavalry, travelling from Trieste, Venice and the Danube to Wagram and Leipzig, and had grown up in French military camps seeing a war every decade. In vain did his mother, Mrs Paraskeva Opujić, send him 'cakes with sad walnuts'. The young Sofronije had his devil born to him before his child. One eye resembled his maternal grandmother's, who had been first and foremost Greek, and the other his father's, who was finally a Serb, and so young Opujić of Trieste saw the world cross-eyed. He would whisper, 'God is who he is and I am who I am not.'

Since early childhood he had carried a big, well-hidden secret. It was as if he felt there was something wrong with him as a human being. And it was natural that he wanted to change that. He wanted to do so badly, secretly, slightly embarrassed by this wish, as if it were an unseemly visit. It was like a small pang of hunger that wails like a pain under the heart or like a small pain that stirs like hunger in the soul. He did not remember exactly when this hidden longing for change had germinated inside him in the form of bodiless energy. It happened as if he had been lying down, putting the tips of his middle finger and thumb together and, having nodded off, his arm slid off the bed and his fingers opened; he woke up with a start as though he had dropped something. In fact he had dropped himself. And the desire was there, this terrible, inexorable desire, so heavy that his right leg began to limp under the weight of it . . . Another time it would seem to him that, once long ago, he had discovered somebody's soul floating in his plate of cabbage and had swallowed it.

And so it was that this secret, powerful thing took seed inside him. It is hard to say whether it was some kind of dizzying ambition connected with his father's military career and his own, some kind of unachievable longing for a new, real enemy and more purposeful alliances; whether young Opujić wanted to reverse his relationship with his father or whether he loved the south and was lured, he of the imperial cavalry, by the fallen empires of the Balkans all the way down to the Peloponnese; whether there was something in the blood of his Greek grandmother whose kin had amassed a fortune in trade between Europe and Asia; or whether it was some other happenstance and desire of the strong and turbid kind that ensures a man's face is never still. One minute it shows what he will look like in old age, the next what he looked like when he still had only his ears to take him through the world. Because a human face breathes, it constantly inhales and exhales time.

Thereafter he worked steadily and prodigiously on bringing some fundamental change to his life, on making his life-long dream come true, but he concealed it as best he could and others often found his actions puzzling.

Since then young Opujić had clandestinely carried a stone under his tongue like a secret or, more to the point, a secret under his tongue like a stone, and his body underwent a change that was difficult to conceal and which gradually entered the realm of legend. It was noticed first by women, but they said nothing; then the men in his regiment began openly joking about it and the story spread all over the battlefield.

'He's like a woman. He can always do it!' the officers in his unit would say with a laugh. From that fateful day on, young Opujić travelled the world carrying his secret inside him and his ever-ready male spear against his stomach. His eleventh finger unbended and started counting the stars. And it stayed that way. That did not bother him. He cheerfully rode his horse but, as for his secret, which might have been the cause of everything, he never said a word to anyone.

'He's fooling around,' the officers in his unit said, as they marched steadily northwestward in the direction of the unknown. He had embarked on this muddy military path at his father's behest, but now he hardly ever met his father, Captain Haralampije Opujić. Sometimes he remembered how at night, in their palace in Trieste, his father would lift his head from the pillow in the dark and listen for as long as could be.

What is he listening to? the boy would wonder in amazement. The house? The war? Time? The sea? The French? His past? Or is he listening to the fear that can be heard from the future? Because the future is a stable out of which steps fear. Then his mother would suddenly lay his father's head back down on the pillow, so that he would not fall asleep stiff-necked and prick-eared. Terrifying to both his subordinates and his superiors, Opujić senior had more love for the son than the mother. And he watched over him from the immense distance of his travelling battlefields. The son had not seen him for a long time and did not know what his father looked like any more or whether he would even recognize him. Let alone his mother in Trieste. It was not in vain that she said of her son, 'That one is a mixture of two bloods, Serbian and Greek. Awake he wants a rainbow, asleep a shop.'

In fact, Lieutenant Sofronije Opujić was like his hounds. He heard and saw behind every corner. He was a veteran soldier; he had been knocked around in the victory at Ulm when he was fourteen and in the defeat in Prussia when he was twenty-two, but somewhere at the bottom of his soul he was still a foolish rascal. He still saw his father behind one corner and heard his mother behind the other. And he longed to meet them. He did not know who he was.

The First Seven Keys

$\mathcal{T}$HE $\mathcal{M}$AGICIAN

'$\mathcal{W}$OULD you like me to breastfeed you, *mon lieu-tenant*?' the girl asked the young Opujić in front of a tent on the outskirts of Ulm.

The lieutenant's eye had been caught by a bird which, in the fast wind above the tent, was flying in place as if tied to it. Inside the tent a male voice was singing 'Memories Are the Sweat of the Soul'. Opujić paid and walked in.

Standing on the table inside was a magician belted with a serpent devouring its own tail and he was singing. He had red roses in his hair. Finishing the song he aimed his high voice over his eyetooth as if targeting the bird above the tent and, like an arrow, his voice felled it. He then offered his services to the visitors. He could eat the name of anyone present for a quarter of a *Napoleon d'or*, and for only slightly more he could eat the surname as well.

'Whoever accepts will never again be called by the same name as the one he walked in with. If you have your house keys, but your house was destroyed by war, I can reconstruct it for you down to the smallest detail simply by tossing the keys into a cauldron, because each key creates an echo giving the ear a clear description of the shape and size of the room that the key guards.'

Finally, the magician proposed that everyone present make a wish and he would help to make it come true, while Mademoiselle Marie would gladly breast-feed each gentleman on his way out to thank him for having come. When it was Opujić's turn to make a wish, the magician became upset, although he had not been informed of his audience's wishes; he quickly stepped down off the table, wanting to slip out of the tent.

There is never enough wisdom in one day, just as there is never enough honey in one flower, thought Opujić and, catching up with the magician, grabbed him by the collar, sat himself down on a barrel and the magician on his knee.

'Stick your tongue out!' he ordered, and the magician quickly obeyed. 'Is it raining?'

The magician nodded his head, even though it was not raining.

'Liar! You think you can fool around with me the way you do with that bird that flies in place above your tent? Do you know who I am?'

'Yes. That's why I wanted to run away. You are the

son of Captain Haralampije Opujić of Trieste.'

'All right. Now to the point. Can you or can you not make a wish come true?'

'Not in your case. But I do know where it can be done. I shall confide something to you. In a temple in Constantinople there is a pillar and attached to it is a copper shield. In the middle of that shield is a hole. Anyone who wants to make a wish must stick his thumb into the hole, close his fist around the thumb so that the fist never leaves the copper surface or the thumb the hole, and his wish will be answered. But take care, sir, and beware. God, when He wants to punish someone, will grant a wish and a terrible misfortune at the same time. Perhaps that is how He treats those He favours, we don't know, but to us it is all the same anyway. So beware, lieutenant. And don't forget the song "Memories Are the Sweat of the Soul".'

'I do not believe a letter of what you are saying,' replied the lieutenant, 'but, all the same, I shall ask you one more question. Can you help me find my father? I haven't seen him since the stone got thin and the wind got heavy. I know that he was retreating toward Leipzig, but I don't know where he is now.'

'That I cannot tell you, but what I can tell you is that a group of pickpockets and charlatans comes to this tent every Thursday to perform for the credulous. They enact the deaths of Captain Haralampije Opujić, your father.'

'What do you mean deaths? He's alive!'

'I know he's alive, lieutenant. But that is what the show is called: *The Three Deaths of Captain Opujić*.'

'I do not believe a word of what you are saying,' said the lieutenant once more and took himself off to bed.

But on Thursday he made some inquiries. In the magician's tent they really were enacting the three deaths of Haralampije Opujić, his father. When young Opujić entered the tent, he asked the first masked actor he could lay his hands on how they dared to portray the death of a living man, but the actor calmly replied, 'You should know that this performance has been paid for personally by Captain Haralampije Opujić himself, who, sir, is a great admirer of the stage and a benefactor of the theatre and comedy. He is now at war on the Elbe.'

Knowing, of course, that the Trieste Opujićes had long been patrons of the theatre, there was nothing else Lieutenant Sofronije could do but sit down and watch the play. When the people in the tent saw him they seemed to go rigid. They had recognized him. He told the actors they were free to begin.

First, a man sporting someone else's beard and a French tunic appeared before them. He played Captain Opujić. Around him stood four women and a girl. One of them turned to the captain and said, 'Just so we immediately know where we stand, please bear in mind that I am not the spirit of your maternal great-grandfather, nor do I represent him in the form of a vampire. He died and nothing of him remains any more, not his body or his spirit. But since deaths do not die, I am here. I am his death. And next to me is the death of your great-great-grandmother. That is all that remains of her. Assuming we understand each other on this point, we can move on. Your ancestors, then, had only one death each. But not you. You will have three deaths and here they are. This old lady here, this lovely woman and this girl here, they are

21

your three deaths. Take a good look at them . . .'

'And that is all that will remain of me?'

'Yes, that is all. And it is not negligible. But, captain, you will not notice your deaths, you will ride through them as you would through the gate of victory and you will continue your journey as though they never happened.'

'But what happens then after my third death, after I become a vampire for the third time?'

'For a while it will seem to both you and others that you are still alive, that nothing happened, until you experience your last love, until you catch the eye of a woman with whom you could have offspring. That same instant you will disappear off the face of the earth, because the third soul cannot have offspring, just as someone who becomes a vampire for the third time cannot have children . . .'

Then the tent went dark and a bear could be heard growling. When the stage lights went back on, a man in a French tunic, embodying Captain Opujić, was wrestling for dear life with a huge bear. The man stabbed the animal with his knife and in its death agony it peed on him and choked him. Both the man and the animal fell to the floor . . .

The audience applauded, the actors gave each spectator a spoonful of boiled wheat for the dead man's soul and someone observed that this was Captain Haralampije Opujić's first death. The second was to follow.

The beautiful woman from Scene One stepped out in front of the audience and said, 'You people do not know how to measure your days. You measure them only in length and say they are twenty-four hours long.

But the depth of your days is sometimes greater than their length and that depth can be a month or even a year long in one day. That is why you do not know how to take stock of your lives. Let alone your deaths . . .'

Upon these words Captain Opujić came riding into the tent, scattering the spectators aside and holding a military field glass in his hand. Appearing behind him, in an Austrian tunic, was a man with a rifle. The Captain turned around and raised the field glass to one eye. That same moment the other man killed him through the field glass. The Captain fell off his horse and the animal, now free of its constraint, galloped off into the night . . . That was Captain Opujić's second death. Again they handed out spoonfuls of boiled wheat for his soul.

Then the little girl from Scene One stepped out in front of the audience and curtsied.

'Don't leave yet. My dead aren't well this evening; stick your finger in my ear so I know you're here even after I fall asleep. Listen! In the darkness the heart beats out somebody's total number of years which are completed inside us . . .'

That heralded the Captain's third and youngest death. On stage (as outside) night had fallen. Two men bearing lanterns and sabres were walking towards one another. It was obviously a duel. One of them portrayed Captain Opujić (in the French tunic); the other the Austrian officer. The one representing Opujić suddenly stopped, stuck his sabre into the ground, hung the lantern on the sabre and moved off into the night, planning to attack the other man from behind. He came up on his opponent in the dark, following the lantern of the man who was standing hesitantly just a few steps away, unable to see what his enemy was up to and why he was standing so still. That moment, when he least expected it, Haralampije Opujić ran straight into the Austrian knife in the dark, far from the sabre and the lantern that the other man had cunningly stuck in the middle of the street. And that was Captain Haralampije Opujić's third death.

I don't understand a thing, the young Opujić thought, leaving the tent.

Just then a voice behind him said, 'It's just as well that you don't understand!'

Turning around, the lieutenant saw the magician with the roses in his hair and asked him, 'What is the truth? Is my father alive or not?'

'Everyone has two pasts,' replied the magician. 'One is called Slowing; this past grows with the person from birth and moves towards death. The other past is called Sliding and it follows the person back to his birth. These two pasts are not of equal length. Depending on which of the two is longer, a person either does or does not fall ill from his death. In the case of the latter it means that the person is building his past on the other side of the grave as well and so it continues to grow even after his death. The truth lies between these two pasts . . . But why doesn't the lieutenant seek out the Papess?' the magician asked in conclusion and left.

KEY 2

The Papess

The Papess was able to read one's every dream in a stranger's tears. She had spent her life in Ulm and had not read fortunes in her youth. She was wont to say, 'Why should I look at someone else's patch of time just to see how someone else's time is tailored? I am not interested in what gentlemen carry in their watches or what time it is under ladies' corsets.'

On a bend of a street, the story goes, she decided to build a little house. As soon as the foundation work was completed, the masons asked her for her cards, told her to shuffle and cross them and under each of the seventy-eight foundation stones of her house they laid a card face down, not looking to see what it was.

It was in this house that one evening the Papess dreamed one of those dreams that last twice as long as the night in which it was dreamed. She was lying in her bed, which had a metal ball on each of its four posts. A man and a beautiful young woman stepped up to her, tied her hair first around her neck and then to the bars of the bed behind her pillow. Then they tilted up the bed, just enough to pull her hair tight. And they said, 'Now we are going to move your house to the sky. For that we need just one good night. We are quick and we are strong. If you do not protest or scream, we shall not touch you. If you do scream, you will see your house in the sky this instant. We won't even move you from your bed.'

She screamed and they tilted up the bed, all the while emptying the house and loading its contents into the wagon. She screamed again, but this time they propped up the bed even more, with her in it, and she was left there to hang by her own hair until morning.

She awoke in her bed, but in a waste land. Overnight and over her living body, thieves had stolen the entire house; they had removed it stone by stone, tile by tile. Not a single window or door handle was ever recovered. Only the bed with its canopy and posts remained intact, but it was propped almost upright against the wall of the house next door, so that she was lying in it half-strangled by her own hair, staring at the ground beneath her feet.

After that she did not want to build a new house but rather preferred to live next door. Meanwhile, out of the foundations of the abducted house grew white roses and red, cypresses, sunflowers, wheat, lilies and palms, and in the middle of the garden grew the Tree of Life and next to it the Tree of Knowledge, and everywhere were wreaths and arches of triumph made of leaves and herbs.

Thereafter the Papess said she had a house in the sky. She kept her canopied bed in the garden and it was there that she read her cards.

It was there that Lieutenant Opujić found her. He walked between the two stones marked black and white and entered the garden.

'Are you the Papess?' he asked the old woman who was there.

'I am the virgin of the Moon,' she replied.

The lieutenant asked her to read his fortune, his and his father's. She told him to come back in the evening. Then she began laying the cards out on her bed. She flipped over the first card and it told her the following:

'Your father belongs to that order of people who are successfully interconnected. In monasteries it is called the order of solidaries – monks who live in a community, eat together and pray together. Here, on the outside, where we live, these people usually hold power; they wage wars. Your father is powerful, has a sabre in his hand and a victorious war under his boots. He and his kind also make excellent doctors, herbalists, singers, masons, viticulturalists, musicians and writers.

'As for you,' the Papess continued, still gazing at the same card, 'you will not belong to their circle, the circle of your father. Pity the victor's son! The world will never be his. And so it is with you. Your father and his brethren will keep you and their other chil-

27

dren in a baby-walker for ever. You will grow old in the cradle. You keep dreaming of your parental home, you prefer female icons to male and will join the order of those solitaries who each live by his own hand and his own hearth. You will eat alone and sleep alone.'

'Just a minute,' said Sofronije. 'In the same card you see one thing for my father and something completely different for me! How can that be?'

'It is simple. One drinks wine and it agrees with him, the other drinks the same wine and it disagrees with him. What do you want?'

'Go on.'

The virgin of the Moon turned over another card and in it saw the following:

'Your father and his kind will support one another like a great holy family; through foreign states they will carry their holy spirit of brotherhood to which all else is subordinated. Your father will have no property because everything he has will be communal, and he will think that means it is also his. His church is their church; that is to say, they themselves will be the church. Your father will prefer day to night and male icons to female. As long as the state that you serve aims for power and plenty, it will belong to your father; and to his kind, his brotherhood.

'As for you, my handsome fellow, you will like wheat and will never become a warrior, rather you will learn the languages of your father's enemies. You will speak well and engagingly and you will therefore also know how to keep silent. You may stay silent for years . . . And another thing. Does your right boot pinch you on occasion?'

'Yes, it does.'

'I thought so. For years under your heart you will carry and hide something big, a dream, a secret or a desire so huge that your right leg will buckle under the weight of it. You will journey far and wide tracking this desire, this hunger which resembles pain, you will roam the roads tracking your pain which pursues this hunger around the world. You will wrestle with it for years. Secretly and alone. Because men like you cannot stand one another. You will have no friends . . . And therefore you will not know who you are.'

'I know perfectly well who I am and what I am,' the lieutenant broke in. 'I am the one who has others spit into my hand when I work and into my plate when I eat. A swallower of knives and the dark, I leap from one stone of madness to another, and my legs do not mean each other well. In one pocket grows wheat, in the other grass. I am exhausted, my soul is coming out of my nose and they are teaching me to sneeze. My father brightens and darkens my sky, it rains in my plate and snows in my bed. I am the one who combs his hair with a fork, the one who sows knives and fattens teeth, because my spoons do not grow when I eat . . . I do not need your lame story.'

'And what do you need, my falcon?'

'That story of yours is a male story. I've heard it before in the monasteries. What about the female part of the story? Do you want to tell me where the woman's place is in your division of roles, or the monastery's or whoever's? Have you forgotten women? Or is the division for men only? I want to know who my mother is, who my sisters are, who my daughters will be.'

'That I cannot tell you. You will get the answer to that question from someone who is a third shoe.'

'What is a "third shoe"?'

'A woman of both sexes.'

'What do you mean?' asked the shocked lieutenant.

'Men have only one sex. Women have two. Beware of the third shoe!'

That same instant, young Opujić again felt under his heart that small pang of hunger which lies silent in the soul like pain. In the garden he felt surrounded by incense, as in a church. He began to read and understand the meanings of the fragrances the way one reads letters. And the fragrances led him down their own path, through the plants in the earth. The lily opened for him like a pure thought untouched by desire, like eternal life, like breastfeeding in a dream, like the sexual organ of a donkey, like clothes beyond the reach of an adult but a towel within the reach of the young. The white rose smelt like Thrace, like Eve before sin, like the sweat of Mahomet, like the human soul and Venus' blood devoid of animal desire, but when that blood painted the rose red, then it smelt of passion, of Eve after sin, of the devil's curse and the Lord's blessing, while the five-leaf rose lashed him with the vital force that belongs to the god of war. The cypress rustled like the holy tree of the goddess of love, it smelt of heaven and of Mount Athos, of flames, of Zeus' sceptre and Amor's arrow, of fragrant fire, and its root smelt

of silver, of gold and of bronze. The wheat smelt of
the body of Christ, Mother Earth, pomegranates and
the underworld, and its echo smelt of salt and wine,
the palm carried victory over death and strength in
movement; the sunflowers looked at him, not at the
Sun, the tree of knowledge behind the old lady's
back offered him its five fruits like five senses, and
the tree of life behind his own back had in lieu of
twelve leaves that same number of small flames that
immediately linked up with the constellation of stars
in the sky and with the pain he carried.

It was then that he saw the Papess begin to turn
over the cards on her bed again: first came the
Magician, then the Hierophant, then the Two of
Wands, the Ace of Pentacles, the Ace of Cups and
Temperance.

'So much for the lily,' she said. She proceeded to
flip over the other cards now. The Fool turned upon
the bed for the white rose, the Magician, the
Hierophant and the Queen of Pentacles for the red
rose, and for the five-leaf rose it was Death. For the
palm, it was the card of the Papess herself, for the
cypress and wheat she flipped over the card of the
Empress, for the sunflower it was the Queen of
Wands and the Sun, and for the tree of love and tree
of knowledge the Papess turned over the cards of the
Lovers and the Chariot.

'Does that mean that the plants have started to
speak the language of the cards that lie under the
foundation of your abducted house?' asked the lieutenant.

'No. For thousands of years now the cards have
been speaking the language of the plants in which

human fate is inscribed. The third shoe is the one that does not step on the plants.'

When he left the garden at dawn, Lieutenant Sofronije Opujić felt as if he was on the edge of a precipice. A hoarse crow flew overhead, its two black wings combing the wind. Suddenly he felt that his loneliness had doubled. Then it began to grow, only to stop for a second and then return to the number two. Someone else was there rusticating in his loneliness. And he decided that for a lonely man that was sheer luck.

ᴛʜᴇ Empress

Oɴ Easter Day 1813, standard-bearer Sofronije Opujić was dispatched on a confidential mission to military headquarters in his section of the war front. His journey took him through Trieste; finally, after so many years, Sofronije saw red earth again and red cattle with the brilliant balls on their horns. He inhaled the bitter sea breeze and spent the night in his parents' house not managing to see his mother that evening.

He was welcomed to the slumbering palace by a beauty with a jewel in her tooth, a sprinkle of stardust in her black hair and an artificial beauty mark between her breasts.

She must be seventeen, thought Sofronije as she

spoke, saying that her name was Petra Alaup, that she was something like his aunt and that Madam Paraskeva, his mother, had instructed her to put him to bed. She led him into a chamber on whose wall hung an icon, a mirror and a painting in an oval gold frame. Opujić was surprised to see that the painting depicted merely a velvet curtain. Petra turned the mirror face against the wall so that it would not attract insects and, without asking, helped young Opujić undress and put him to bed like a child. Seeing his eleventh finger standing erect, she observed, 'Madam Paraskeva says you cannot go to church like that tomorrow.'

Then she sat down by the lamp and began to knit.

'Are you hungry?' she asked, laughing into her knitting.

Opujić laughed too and said, 'I have the name of a fish. All I need is a fish and I am full. But it is not for everyone.'

'Look at him!' retorted Petra. 'Now he wants it all and would give anything to get it, but as soon as he gets it he falls asleep on top of you and fills your mouth with mucus from who knows what kind of dirty dream, where they give him what he would never get in real life. You can barely pull yourself out from under him. Here is the skein, you hold it until you fall asleep. Just be careful you don't break the thread. If it breaks, then the person I am knitting this for will plunge downstream.'

'And what is that you are knitting?'

'I gathered strands of hair and am knitting a prick-cosy.'

'For whom?'

'Certainly not for you; I haven't measured you.'

At that moment Petra stopped knitting and placed her beautifully chiselled hand upon her breast.

'O woe is me,' she whispered.

'What's the matter?'

'I have a visitor.'

'What kind of visitor?'

'A small pain under my heart, which moans like a small pang of hunger. Or better yet, I have a small pang of hunger which craves pain.'

'One might say that you have already had a visitor, because the pain and hunger at the bottom of your soul usually come after a visit, or I'm not the man with a white beard in this black one! I know which glass not to refill with wine.'

'O woe is me! Which glass?'

'A full one, as well you know.'

'You don't know a thing. Your brains work only in your ears. Do you know how many of them have spent the night under this hair?'

'No.'

'Well, neither do I. But I know I was born with this hunger.'

With these words Petra walked over to the window, plucked a blade of porcupine grass from the flowerpot and put it in her mouth, tied it into a knot with her tongue and showed the knot to Sofronije.

'Done! It doesn't hurt any more . . . And you? I would say you have not tried female bread yet, have you? You're simply not seeing through your third eye, are you? Now, now, don't be afraid. Even a watch that has stopped eventually arrives at the correct time. Come on, I'll teach you how to pray with four hands

35

if you solve something for me.'

'What?'

'Guess what my left tit is called?'

' I don't know.'

'And the right one?'

'I know!' Then Opujić the standard-bearer whispered something in the dark.

'That's right!' Petra giggled, grabbed the guitar off the wall and held it out to him.

'I don't know how to play.'

'I am not asking you to. Toss a silver coin inside and come in.'

Sofronije then decided to play his last card. He pressed his hand under his chest and moaned.

'What's the matter? Have you got a visitor too? A pain under your heart which moans like a small pang of hunger?'

'It's not that.'

'What is it then?'

'I don't have a silver coin.'

'You miser!' said Petra as she turned the mirror around to face the room and the icon to face the wall and then lay down in Sofronije's bed. On each breast she had something like a little pear.

'You may not have a silver coin, but your mother has,' she said in a mute whisper lip to lip.

'Peep, peep, peep, my pretty ones, be wise and don't believe every wind that comes your way!'

These were the words that woke up the young Lieutenant Opujić in the middle of his house in Trieste on the Wednesday of St Martin-the-Confessor.

'Peep, peep, peep, my pretty ones,' said a deep

voice sounding as if it came from a cunt. 'May the candlestick be the one in a thousand that is yours! Wolves devour counted sheep too, you know. Peep, peep, peep, my pretty ones. Don't cross to the joyless side, to the black shoulder, from the shore of prosperity and measure to the shore of sand and wind, where all weight and value disappears like the price of a cap without a head. But beware of the other side too! Take care that this soldier son of mine, who has darkness growing between his eyes and kisses between his teeth, does not step over to your side. He will attack you where not even a rash would dare . . . Peep, peep, peep, my pretty ones . . .'

A large woman was bending over the bed, her hair streaked with grey, but since the grey hairs did not grow as fast as the black, her grey locks were noticeably shorter. She looked at him with eyes speckled like a serpent's egg. Even before he lifted open his eyelids, Sofronije could smell her almond fragrance and he recognized his mother. Leaning over the bed with her were four or five women in rustling hooped dresses and a bald young man with a black moustache.

'Get up, you lazybones, it's time to go to church!' his mother twittered, turning the icon back to face the room. 'What does a hen peck? Seeds. And what pecks away at the hour? Hiccups, my lovely. Listen, that one keeps pecking and hiccuping one and the same thing: Now! Now! Now!'

Madam Paraskeva suddenly whisked the cover off her son and the women. Seeing him naked and protruding, she shrieked.

'I'll kill that Petra! How can you go to church like that?' exploded Madam Paraskeva, grabbing her ears

37

with crossed hands.

The Church of St Spiridon was full and one could see that it was sinking at one end, because the bottom edge of the icons on the southern side had separated slightly from the wall. The church had been built on marshland. In the middle of the service someone stepped on Sofronije's spur and he turned around to see Petra in black, flashing her smile with the precious jewel inside.

'Look,' she said drawing his attention. 'The one standing by the icon of St Alimpije, the one who wraps her hair around her neck, that is your sister Sara. She wears a ring under her tongue to fool her hunger and wears socks instead of gloves in the evening because she has no one to warm her. The one standing next to your mother, the one who can be girdled by a strand of hair, is your sister-in-law Anica. You can pour a glass of wine between her breasts and drink it without spilling a drop. Next to her is your sister-in-law Martica, who screws as easily as she cries. If you dream about her, turn your pillow over and she will dream about you. The bald one over there, that's her husband, your brother Luka. He is holding a rock in his hand right now so as not to doze off in church. If he falls asleep the rock will drop out of his hand and wake him up. Your mother says he holds the rock even in bed when he is screwing Martica . . .'

'Now for some drunken bread,' said Madam Paraskeva Opujić, sitting down at a table for twelve, 'and then we can see our eyes reflected in the soup. This is what I say to them, to those heretics, about you, Lord, you who bring luck to my door. When I ride a wagon, I praise the owner and the horse! Oh

Lord, have mercy on Mr Haralampije, our master and mine, wash clean his hands and ours, before Thy bread and Thy blood, oh Lord, because Thy hands are always clean and Thou dost not take verbs into them. In taking care of Thyself, oh Lord, takest care of me and of all that is Haralampije's. Amen.'

When they sat down, Madam Paraskeva took a crust of bread and stuck it under her belt.

'Look, son, at your sisters and at your brothers and their wives, your sisters-in-law. They spend six months of the year in the month of June, and December enters their house barely once. And all this was given them by your father Haralampije. Just look at Marta: pie's grandchildren dipped in hot aromas; look at Marko, pork sprinkled with sugar and then roasted and cabbage pickled on St Luke's Day; you, Sara, take some pillow-like dough; you, Luka, are fondest of fish's sisters-in-law done in hot wine; you, children, take my two- and three-winged doves . . . Just look at it, just taste the beauty of it! All sweet arse-melting and pants-filling delights, they warm, they prickle, they leap around your teeth, they defend themselves, they pee under the tongue, they bite behind the ear and spread wherever they pass. They change their minds and go for the nose. And when they depart, they leave traces: a memento that pleases and kisses you as if you were a little icon . . . And you, Anica, put a clove of garlic in your ear to ward off the devils, because they are as close to you as they are to this menace of mine, Sofronije, who drank to quench someone else's thirst and dined to sate someone else's hunger. Do you know what is sweetest to eat, Sofronije?'

'No, Mother.'

'Your father's house. You nibble happily at the doorposts and door handles, at the windows and doorsteps, and all you spit out is the key.'

'I don't need Father's house, Mother.'

'Listen to him! Cooked in honey, taught by the jug. While for us here it's: Don't stop! Keep moving! I think I know what you need. You need a wife. And the bracelet for her is inside this little pouch.'

Sofronije's brother Marko quickly handed over the little silk pouch in which Sofronije saw the gold bracelet and its inscription, which began with the words: 'I am an amulet . . .'

'Thank you, Mother. But I do not intend to marry.'

'And what am I supposed to do? Am I to fall ill from your youth while you recover from it? You don't need a house, you don't need a wife. But I need your wife, and your sisters need a house. Jovana has no dowry unless this house of ours becomes her dowry. But I have you up my sleeve like a fool of a joker and I will get you married even if it means washing my face with tears! You saw Petra in church, she won't go with either a male cross or a female, but she has as many vineyards as ships and is capable of weighing the flames of a fire. Take her. She will salt your fire and tame your fork. Then we will give Jovana half our palace as a dowry and she will be able to choose a groom. If you don't, she won't be able to choose. She will take someone old but rich. So, you choose.'

'Or guess,' said Sofronije's sister-in-law Marta, breaking into the conversation, upon which Anica burst into laughter and added, 'Was this capon roasted on a male or a female tree?'

'I don't want you, Mother, to get me married on a

capon,' said Sofronije.

'Listen, my son, do you know how I got married? One night I bit my tongue in my sleep. The next night I did it again, I already had a sore on my tongue. I wondered what I could be saying at night to keep biting my tongue like that. I combed through all the words that I know in my mind and – I found it! I found the one word that fit the sore on my tongue the way a scabbard fits the sabre. "Trieste!" I cried, jumping into the first carriage and coming straight here and straight into Haralampije Opujić's arms. I remember it as if it was yesterday. I met him at a party and wanted to dance with him. The girls told me he was taken. "What do you mean taken?" I asked, and they laughed, led me to a small window and told me to take a peek. I looked and there was Haralampije locked in a room with a live bear, and when he killed it with his knife the bear, in its agony, peed all over him. We laughed a lot and were in love a lot and that same year of 1789, in the depth of winter, I had you, Sofronije. That is how one does it . . . You just go on eating, my falcon, just keep eating and don't worry. The quicker the teeth, the quicker the ears. As for what you are going to do, don't tell me, tell your sister Jovana. I am already baking the wedding rolls. They throb under my fingers like your father's drums. Inside each, two yolks jiggle like two little breasts, and when you take a bite they breathe! . . . To your health!'

That evening Sofronije entered his room alone and stretched out on his bed without turning on the light. Next to the icon and mirrors on the wall hung that gold-framed oval painting of the velvet curtain, but

41

now he noticed there a fine pair of breasts, so well depicted that they looked real. Gold dust glittered in the blonde hair, and, true to the latest fashion, the breasts were bare, with only a transparent veil to cover them. The nipples were painted the same colour as the lips. Everything looked so real that Sofronije walked up and in disbelief reached out to touch the finely painted breasts. And in the semi-darkness his fingers got smacked.

'Don't touch that!' said the portrait. 'I am your sister Jovana, and this is not a painting, it is the window of my room. As for you, Brother, sir, thank you for what you have given me and for what you have not given me. I keep my earthly servant, my body, in my soul. And it obeys me. See how obedient it is . . .'

And, leaning her elbows on the frame of her window, Jovana burst into tears. 'And when, Brother, sir, you get angry with me and assail me for years as if with stones, the Virgin descends from the Amperian sky above to the heavenly draft where the birds fly, and she weeps for me. Taking milk in her two glass bottles and lighting the flame in her icon lamps, with a black violet under her robes, she slowly sets out to meet her groom and her fate. And everything obediently serves her: the glass bottles and the icon lamps and the flower, and she has her earthly servant, her body. And so Mercy and Truth meet. And I cannot take refuge either with her or with you.'

Standing at her little window, Jovana burst into even louder sobs. Sofronije came over and began to stroke her, and she touched his hair and said, 'It has grown long. Come, let me trim it.'

And she pulled him through the window. Sofronije

sat in the middle of the room, his sister placed an earthenware pot in his lap, took a knife from the shelf, sharpened it on the fork, stepped up to her brother, put the knife between her teeth and began to comb him with the fork. When she finished she stuck the pot on his head and began to clip around it as if he were a sheep. A drop fell on his hand.

'Is that rain?'

'Yes, it is rain.'

'No, it is not rain, it is you crying. Do you really love him so much?'

'I see, Brother, that it is not the body that gives birth to the soul. It seems our souls do not come from the same earthly parents as our feet, they do not come from Haralampije and Paraskeva, they come from different springs, each following its own wave in life and seeking its own ears, so that brother and sister do not hear each other and our souls are not of the same family, they are not related in the same way as our hands. Where did your soul come from? We created a flower in our dreams, but what actually sprang up was a thistle. The one I am waiting for is of quiet voice and costly truth.'

'He must have a big head but a brain like yours,' said Sofronije angrily, removing the pot from his head. 'Who is he?'

'My brother in soul and my husband in body. His name is Pana Tenecki; he is from Zemun. I don't know him well yet. I just know that he exists, and that I can't sleep from the beauty of him . . . He will come to see me this evening . . . Now stay still so I don't nick you.'

Jovana put the pot back on her brother's head and resumed clipping.

'He will pass through your room. You won't tell on us, will you?' she asked.

'No, I won't,' said Sofronije, deciding to go to sleep as soon as he lay down. But to his astonishment, somewhere around midnight a man in an Austrian officer's tunic passed through his room, and soon afterwards he heard whispering through the window in the gold frame. A female voice, the voice of Sofronije's sister, said, 'You frightened me. A person can fall asleep even when weeping . . .'

'Why were you weeping?'

'The man I am being offered is old and I'm not. How can I marry him? If my father were here he would protect me from my mother. He loves me. And you? Advise me what to do.'

'No.'

'Why not?' replied the pleading female voice in the dark.

'Because there is no advice. Everyone must eat his own path like a worm.'

'So, there is no help to be had.'

'Who was talking about help? The help I can offer you exists. It is fast and it is efficient, but I don't know if you would like it.'

'Why not?'

'Because it is the kind of help that cannot be corrected later.'

'What do you mean?'

'I don't mean anything. My help is not to mean but to do.'

Just then Sofronije heard a man's heavy belt fall to the ground, its chains clanging.

'Then do something, for God's sake, before it's too

late! Save me!' the woman's small voice whispered back.

'I don't dare.'

'Why not?'

'You'll scream.'

'I'll scream? Why would I scream? If this mouth were mute then your love would be deaf.'

'The saying is: receive my blood and my body and I shall sacrifice myself for you and redeem you. Just have faith in me. But you do not believe that it hurts.'

'That what hurts?'

'My help. At least the first time . . . Can your blouse be unbuttoned with the tongue?'

'Why with the tongue?'

'Because as long as it is buttoned I cannot help you . . .'

At that moment Sofronije Opujić silently began to dress. As he was pulling on his boots, he heard his sister's last words; a whisper which never rose to a scream, 'Help! I'm being attacked! Oh, sir, don't do that to me, please! Help! You're heavy, get off me, I can't breathe, why are you pressing so hard? . . . You're pricking me. Not there, it tickles . . . you're so hairy, what are you doing? You'll choke me with that drool! Get off, it's dripping into my mouth . . . You'll bite that off, leave it! You're pinching me . . . Help, murderer! . . . Is that blood and body? . . . Oh, sir, don't do that . . . don't do that . . . do that . . . Oh, sir, please . . .'

Standard-bearer Sofronije Opujić crept out of his own house as quietly as a thief. In the entrance hall a burning candle was stuck into the navel of a small loaf of bread, and arrayed on the silver tray were Easter eggs. He picked one up, it was as big as if a rooster had laid it, quickly saddled his horse and wearing the parade uniform of the French cavalry rode straight to Petra's house. He woke her up, gave her the egg, said he had come to say goodbye and asked her:

'Tell me, what is the connection between us Opujićes and the Teneckis of Zemun?'

'Don't you know? It began in the last war and in the last century. In 1797 with the collapse of the Venetian state. Your father met Pahomije Tenecki, the father of this Pana Tenecki who is now screwing your sister.'

'What kind of relationship do they have?'

Petra kissed him goodbye and in her kiss told him in a mute whisper, lip to lip, 'It couldn't be worse.'

Sofronije rode north-west and felt he had a visitor. A small hunger was moaning under his heart like an unquenched desire, or was it a weak pain whimpering inside him like hunger?

KEY 4

$\mathcal{T}$HE $\mathcal{E}$MPEROR

$\mathcal{P}$AHOMIJE Tenecki was of the Teneckis who had produced two excellent painters in two generations. He was of the Teneckis who knew that Velazquez had twenty-seven shades of black. They had come to Zemun in 1785 with Georgije Tenecki, who had been commissioned to paint the portraits of the famous Karamats. Pahomije Tenecki, from the lateral branch of the family, was half Polish on his mother's side. His gift for music probably came from her. Although he had inherited the bell foundry in Zemun, he preferred going to Budim to learn to play music.

While still a child, at an age when the dead had not yet entered his dreams, Tenecki made an unusual decision. He played the clarinet extremely well and at

47

one moment the pleasure it gave him awoke in him such a hunger for life that he decided, to everyone's surprise including his own, to live for as long as long could be. For ever and a day, as the saying goes. He did not know how to do this, no one could tell him the secret, but Pahomije felt an absolute determination and irrepressible desire to subjugate everything to this goal. He wondered whether the body went first or the soul. He had heard that the 'for ever' of the familiar saying referred to the soul and 'a day' to the body. And, a priest had told him, it was easier to lose the 'for ever' than 'a day' in this complex calculation, which now preoccupied him so.

Later, when he grew up, Pahomije Tenecki studied music in Vienna, developed feet which were always as hot as live coal, so that his shoes smoked in the rain, and an icy hand, the right one, which he used in lieu of a beer glass to cool his cheeks. He adored the compositions of Paisiello and could divide his memories of Zemun, Pest and his parents into hot memories and cold. He was already married, with two sons – Pana and Makarije – and a daughter Jerisena, when a friend happened to toss out a sentence that changed Pahomije Tenecki's life.

'Those who have killed the most, live the longest . . .'

Pahomije Tenecki immediately began to practise. Not the clarinet any more or Paisiello and Haydn. Now what he practised was target shooting. Admittedly, he did for a while hesitate between music and the army, but the matchless dexterity of his fingers, practised for years on the clarinet, suddenly proved to be extremely useful here as well. It enabled Tenecki to become one of the best marksmen in

Vienna. And that was not all. Memories cold and hot, a cold hand and a hot hand, were made to order for Pahomije Tenecki's new skill. These traits gave that skill an extraordinariness and, even more important when it came to the matter of guns, an unpredictability. At the rifle range where he practised people began to fear and avoid him.

'He shoots as if he were playing the clarinet,' they whispered. 'It is hard to get the better of a man like that.'

Indeed it was. As soon as another war broke out, in which the French destroyed the Republic of Venice in 1797, Pahomije Tenecki clipped his seven-year-old moustache, packed away his rifle in its velvet-lined box as if putting away his clarinet and signed up with the Austrian army. He was immediately sent off to the battlefield and in one of his first engagements he demonstrated his marvellous skill with a gun and saved, or rather captured, a dark-haired girl from a cellar. He dragged her around with him thereafter. He knew nothing about her, not even whether she understood his language or whether she was literate, although he suspected not. Instead of saying something to her that first day, he slapped her, because a word can be left unheard but a slap never. And that is how they communicated from the very beginning, without much conversation.

She kept stubbornly silent, ate little and grew more and more beautiful. He did not know her name, and he did not know her religion. He did not know whether she was a virgin or not, because he did not make love to her. But every evening, some time around 'white darkness', he made her suck him. The

49

girl painted the inner shells of her ears blood-red with her lip rouge and did what he asked of her, lightly touching him with her fingers and lips, showing no signs of either attraction or repulsion. As time passed, these seances became longer and longer and more and more unusual. Sometimes this touching and these embraces seemed to remind Tenecki of something, but he never knew what. Anyway, he did not have the time to rack his brains over such matters. With a dismissive wave of his hand he reasoned that the fate of a woman was always decided by a 'Yes' and the fate of a man by a 'No'. The war against France was raging and Pahomije Tenecki quickly made a name for himself. Soon, a clearing the length of a rifle range formed around him, like the one in Vienna. On both sides of the firing line, everyone was afraid of him. And he did what he wanted. If the sentence he had heard in his youth was correct, then his life-span was growing substantially longer by the day . . . But then his superiors told him:

'This job is not for you. You have no equal here, no one to compete against. You will turn soft and lose your skill. What kind of report is this? Judge for yourself: "And we fought from six in the morning until ten o'clock, driving some into the water and drowning them, some we slayed in the woods, some we killed in the trees, and some escaped and from them we got ten standards and trumpets." Is that work for someone like you? There are others who can do that. Now you go and pack. On another front, slightly further north from here, you will find someone who is your equal, if not even better than you. But beware; he is on the other side, on the French side. Go and take care of him.'

And so Pahomije Tenecki took his rifle box, his spy-glass and the girl by the hand and departed. But he could find neither hide nor hair of the other man. There was no one who could match Tenecki. Here again Pahomije did as he pleased in the battlefield and spent his nights with the girl. One afternoon a strange thing happened. He was attacked by an unarmed merchant, Jeremije Kaloperović by name, who tried to injure him. Tenecki did not want to kill the man; he merely wounded him in the arm. Despite the injury, the man kept weaving frantically around the battle-field, following Tenecki from afar. He wept as he saddled up an ivory-embellished black box and bribed the soldiers to get it to Miss Rastina.

'Who is this Rastina woman?' a surprised Tenecki asked his men.

'What do you mean who is she? She is the woman with whom you, captain, now choose to live. She is the fiancée of the said merchant from Karlovci, Kyr Kaloperović.'

Tenecki burst out laughing and left to spend yet another night with Rastina. That was when he discovered that she might have the perfect *embouchure*, as musicians of the Vienna school called the mouth's grip on a wind instrument. He tried to keep his mind on that. Rastina still stubbornly kept silent, but once more they were cut short by the dirty little war. His old unit was calling him back. The man on the French side had appeared in their sector of the battlefield. Obviously, he was looking for Tenecki. And so Tenecki returned to his old unit, and Rastina finally spoke:

'Whom the devil are we looking for all this time?' she asked.

51

'Well, well, the little dove has cooed,' replied Tenecki. 'And she has cooed just when she should. You want to know about that other man? The one who is after my head? Well, then, listen carefully.

'The man we are looking for is called Haralampije Opujić. The Opujićes are rich, they are merchants from Trieste and they are Serbs. This one is a captain, he has the best horse on this flank of the French army, he has his silverware carried behind him in a leather trunk, and he carries his little knife and fork handily below his belt, in the same sheath. He supports his own travelling theatre, which performs scenes from his life and, bizarrely, depicts his deaths even though he is alive. He is known to be loved by women. But he likes a soft cunt, his fingers always smell of a woman and he is not easy to satiate. The mother loves him more than her husband, the wife loves him more than her son, and the daughters love him more than their brothers and more than they will ever love any man. He is robust and quick. He can slap a fish out of water with his paw like a bear. He crosses himself quickly as if catching a fly, and he draws his strength and health from women's milk. They hire wet-nurses for him as if he were a child, and the women who cushion his ears at night make him cheese from their milk. And in the morning one of them empties her breast on a brush with which he later cleans his teeth. After making love he does not get up until he has smoked a pipe of tobacco. He never takes his mistresses with him on his campaigns, but one of them is always waiting for him somewhere by the Danube. Now Haralampije Opujić, the one we are after, is lying in the dark in that tower facing ours, his head resting on his fists, thinking. His thoughts make the blood curdle or at least catch the breath of someone sleeping off in the distant darkness. But not mine. I am not afraid. I see when the crow turns grey in mid-flight.

'But Captain Opujić is made of solid stone himself. From the Rhine to the Neva, from Wargam to the Danube, he has seen his fill of bird nests made of female hair and has fought his share of battles, first in the Austrian and now in the French army.

'As for his deaths, I have seen them in the theatre and at the fair and know all about them. Captain Opujić is difficult to approach. For instance, he drinks brandy made with twenty-four herbs but is never drunk. If the alcohol does slightly get to him, he takes an onion, squeezes it in his hand until it releases its juice and then smells it. That quickly dispels the hangover and clears his head. He knows that there is no love among nations but there is hate. He is fond of saying that victory has many fathers but defeat is always an orphan; however, he also thinks, albeit never says, that both defeat and victory always have the same mother. He knows that I, like everyone else, hate my own livelihood most. But above all he is an able soldier. Nine horses have dropped under him in battle so far. And with his rifle he can kill a carp when it leaps out of the river. He is feared both by his own people and by his enemies. I heard that a French major had given him offence, he had wanted to poke fun at him or something. Opujić said nothing and swallowed the insult; he even accompanied the major to the residence the latter had requisitioned in the town of Ulm on the Danube. The Frenchman slept well that night, but when morning came neither house nor homestead was standing there. Overnight Opujić's men had stolen the entire house over the major's living body. Not a single brick was to be found. Standing there alone in the waste land was just the major's canopied bed, in the bed was an old woman and under the bed was a stack of cards. But not a trace of the major himself.

'It is also rumoured that Captain Opujić is turning deaf. In a strange way, too. The better his son Sofronije Opujić hears below ground, they say, the worse the father hears here above ground. And the former is reportedly growing and hearing better and better. Hence Captain Opujić's saying: "Everything, if it is really to be heard, has to be said at least twice."

'That, then, is the emperor who lies there in the opposite tower, waiting and watching for me through the dark and the stars, just as I am for him.'

THE HIEROPHANT

CAPTAIN Tenecki and Rastina lay alone in the tower on the battlefield. In war Tenecki was always alone. On one wall of the chamber was a painting of a ship in a storm and, before falling asleep, Rastina looked at that sea in the moonlight and was afraid that the painted water would make her pee in her bed, as she used to when she was a child. Hanging on the other wall was a painting of a woman seized by a centaur who, trotting off with her thrown across his back, turned his head around to suckle her breast and be nursed by her. According to the caption under the painting, he was an Eleusinian hierophant and the woman riding him represented the world. This hierophant sucked mercy from one of the woman's breasts and severity from the other, from one he sucked law and from the other the liberty to obey or disobey. To Rastina it was as if this master of the sacred mysteries, this emperor who transformed himself into a hierophant, this centaur, was lurking outside in the dark, waiting for the moment when he could show Tenecki his sacred fiery object and suck Rastina's milk.

At any rate, the two peerless marksmen finally confronted each other. They took up positions in the two facing towers at a distance of an eighth of a rifle-range apart. Both thought that this would be the beginning of weeks of wearing each other down, but it took only a day.

White darkness was falling. Tenecki was lying in the attic, gazing at the roof above him as if at an inverted ship, sensing and watching the tower below him, drinking in the smells that were becoming vampires. Then he descended. He could feel Rastina, her fingers and lips on his body. And he thought that in its unending variety her touch lasted an eternity, as if 'for ever'. And then suddenly he stopped feeling her touch and began listening to it. For the first time he heard Rastina's lips and fingers from within, through himself. And then finally he understood. Through all the battles, through the fall of Venice, through the two changes of battlefields, Rastina had been playing Franz Joseph Haydn not on the clarinet but inside him, inside Austrian Captain Pahomije Tenecki. At the moment she was performing 'Allegro con spirito' from Haydn's *Divertimento – Corale di Sant' Antonio per lauto, oboe, clarinetto, fagotto e corno*, her lips and fingers faultlessly mastering Haydn's composition. Pahomije Tenecki decided that the girl's clarinet playing put

Tenecki's own skills, along with Paisiello's, to shame. He looked in amazement at the girl on top of him and he came just when she was moving on to the 'Minuetto'. But then the dirty little war interfered once more. Tenecki smelt the smoke, swore and thought to himself: Never enough time for eternity! And he ran to the window. There, in the middle of the night, he could clearly see the smoke gathering from the neighbouring tower, the one Captain Opujić had shut himself into. Tenecki could not believe his own eyes. Opujić's tower was on fire. Now he had to think quickly. If the tower really was on fire, the other man could either burn with it or jump out of the exit right within sight of Tenecki's rifle.

Soon the flames appeared on the floor above as well. Something unbelievable was happening. Tenecki grabbed his spyglass and began carefully watching the exit from the tower, stepping slightly out from behind his screen to do so. It was then that the eye in his spyglass and the eye in his head were pierced by a single shot from Captain Opujić, only a second before he jumped out of the blaze he himself had lit.

Into the tower where the shot Tenecki lay soon came a man, so heavy he could have carried the church bell, holding a rifle and dressed in the sumptuous attire of the French cavalry. He ran over to the dead Tenecki, kicked away his rifle and felt an irresistible urge to piss all over the downed enemy. But when he saw the terrified girl cowering in a corner of the tower, he renounced his intention, embraced her and began to comfort her gently. He whispered as if in prayer, 'What is this now, Lord? Why pour brandy on the fire, oh Lord? Why not be a God who walks in front of us, not behind us? Thou hast deceived me but not out-witted me. Why salt our open seas and waste so much salt and water, oh Lord? Where art thou leading us?'

He then spoke to Rastina, all the while stroking her hair, 'Come, my child, do not be afraid, your brother and fiancé are waiting for you down below. They have turned grey with worry.'

As they stepped out of the tower and into the night two apparitions were indeed waiting for them. Rastina's brother and her fiancé Jeremije Kaloperović. Her brother was carrying a rifle and Jeremije a black ivory-encrusted box, inside of which was Rastina's clarinet. But Rastina did not even glance their way. Without a word she took the black box from her fiancé and walked off into the darkness after Captain Opujić. Turning around in surprise, the latter said, 'Where are you going, my child? My moustache is older than you. Be careful.'

'I want to have your child. You gave me life, I shall give it back to you. A life for a life.'

And she refused to be parted from him. At the first inn, during dinner at the World's Navel Tavern, the captain fasted on lentils and brandy. And he did not relax at all. A beggar woman entered the tavern, wearing a man's cap and shouting 'Let this cap be filled by women who have never cheated on their men! But only by them! Let no one else wave their arms and reach out for it . . .'

Rastina tore a silver button off her blouse and tossed it into the cap. The captain laughed and took her off with him to bed. As they left he muttered, 'You know, Tenecki miscalculated. He thought and believed that the more people he killed the longer he would live. But, in truth, that is nonsense. The point lies not there: one never knows who killed whom – the victor the vanquished or the vanquished the victor. Tenecki is now lying in that tower and birds have already started alighting on him as if he were a branch, and he does not know that it was perhaps I who was killed, not he . . .'

Seeing that the captain was as skittish as his two-year-old mare, Rastina showered him with kisses and wanted to whisper something into his ear, but he closed her mouth with his hand.

'Do not worry, my dear, I know that you had others before me. It does not matter. I shall deflower you all the same.'

And he prodded her clitoris with his blindman's rod in such a way that it tore both lips under her belly. She wept and said into his ear, 'You will have to do it once more.'

When Captain Opujić lay down on top of her for the second time, he realized with surprise that Rastina was a virgin.

$\mathcal{T}$HE $\mathcal{L}$OVERS

$\mathcal{W}$HEN Rastina Brunswick returned to Sremski Karlovci from the battlefront in 1797, because Captain Opujić could not keep taking her from one battle to the next, she immediately sought out Jeremije Kaloperović, her ex-fiancé. He bore a scar on his hand from the gun of the late Pahomije Tenecki and had tiny stars of grey in his beard.

'If you want a woman who has thrice lost her virginity, who despises you and who will bear you another man's child, then take me,' she told Kyr Jeremije. He thought to himself: One's own pain is merely the reverberation of someone else's, and he took her.

Rastina Brunswick thus got married in Karlovci and moved into the spacious Kaloperović house in

Sugar Lane. She first had a son, Arsenije, and then a daughter, Dunja.

Rastina's husband never showed any signs of impatience, but sometimes his sentences would strangely skip ahead of themselves when he spoke, because he always wanted to say two things at the same time. He told the children that there were fish in the sea that could only stand a certain amount of salt in the water. If the water had more salt than they could bear, the fish would become dazed. And the same is true of us. Because human happiness is like salt. Too much of it leaves us dazed.

Master Kaloperović bought Rastina and Dunja fish-skin hats and a subscription to the *Serbian Newspaper of the Imperial City of Vienna*. Dunja grew into a thin, gluttonous little girl. Into every opening she had, she shoved whatever she could lay her hands on – spinning tops, grasshoppers, buttons, live fish, hairpins, beans, snails and balls, carrots, eggs, pea pods, bottles of Cologne water, cucumbers and marbles, Venetian almanacs and pencils, door handles and musical watches and finally a fish bladder that burst inside her . . .

Master Kaloperović sent the boy to school.

'Let him be like Cicero.'

And so young Arsenije Kaloperović went to the Serbian-Latin School of Karlovci and on the very first day brought home a most unusual person, as lovable as a kitten, already full of Latin quotes and pretty as a doll. This male doll was called Avksentije Papila; he was Arsenije's school-mate and distantly related to some demoted general. An orphan without any means, Papila looked better in his friends' old clothes

61

than they did in their new. He carried the birthmark of a small wound on his temple, which gave him a mysterious look.

'He of the bruised head,' his friends used to joke, but they loved him. He was the favourite of all the cats, all the priests' wives and all the pupils in Karlovci. For that or some other reason, wherever Papila went he would be the object of some incredible, often ghastly story. The best part of it all was that he himself never heard any of these stories and was always terribly surprised if anyone ever told him one. Only occasionally did he feel that his life's path was curling up ahead of him like a worm.

The boys had already advanced to rhetoric class. Papila spent more time in the spacious Kaloperović house than in his own miserable abode, and one evening he began to transcribe for himself and for Arsenije the manuscript of a textbook he had borrowed from another pupil. He wrote in his fine handwriting, dipping the pen into his mouth and into the inkpot in turns, and saying out loud: '*Praecepta artis oratoriae in tres partes digesta et Juventuti Illyrico-Rasciane tradita ac explicata in Collegio Slavono-Latino Carloviciensi, Anno Domini. . .*'

Suddenly a little mirror was shoved in front of his eyes. Madam Rastina giggled, pointing to the ink spot, and she wiped his lips with her perfumed sleeve.

'Will you teach Dunja and me Latin? Time passes slowly for us like this.'

'I will,' said Papila, 'if you will take me to the theatre in Temisoara and if Master Jeremije will order a book for me as well.'

'Which one would you like?'

'The one about Eladie, who sold his soul to the devil, by Vikentije Rakić and a German book about Doctor Faustus. Both were printed in 1808.'

Thus started the Latin lessons in the house of Master Kaloperović, which was clearly visible from the ships sailing down the Danube. Avksentije Papila gave Miss Dunja her lessons on the veranda first, and then they would move into the drawing room together with Arsenije, whose mother occasionally liked to lick his hair down with her spit. It was here that Latin began to work its spell on Madam Rastina. It was here that fritters stuffed with wild snails were brought on to the table, along with a pie made of spices presented in a faience dish. At the bottom of the dish was a network of little gutters that led like arteries to a small heart-shaped hole. This heart collected the oil so that the fritters would not swim in their own grease. The pie was served with nettle tea mixed with honey, the favourite beverage of the young Master Papila, who then taught Madam Rastina rhetoric or read out sections from the *Iliad*, purring like a cat:

Behind the seas, near Troy, lies a water which is bitter and unpotable. Thirsty animals gather at this watering place, but they cannot drink until the unicorn arrives. His horn is medicinal and when he lowers his head to drink, the horn stirs the water, making it murky but sweet to drink. And then the other thirsty animals drink alongside him. And when he quenches his thirst and lifts his horn out of the water, the water becomes as bitter as it was before. But while the unicorn is stirring the water with his horn, he clears it further with his eyes and visible in that clearness, as if laid out in the palm of one's hand, is the future . . .

One evening when Arsenije did not attend class, just when Papila was about to interpret for her a new chapter – 'De Tropis Dictionis' – his pupil and guardian, Madam Rastina, said: 'I have something to tell you, my beauty. Madam Avakumović confided to me a secret which is worth hearing. Now listen. Some sixteen years ago a child was to be born into a family of a celebrated name. It is true that the mother dreamed she would have a son, and the father dreamed he would have a daughter, but neither ever dreamed that the child would have a different father. And so the expected child became an unwanted child. The mother had to remove it before her husband suspected anything. The sorceress she had summoned told her that this could best be done if the embryo was transferred to another person or even to an object. The story does not say how this was to be achieved, but sure enough the embryo was transferred to a soft velvet armchair with ears. The embryo continued to grow inside the armchair and one day, when her husband stretched himself out in the armchair, there was a crunching sound . . .'

Here the young Papila suddenly interrupted the lady's story and, quite confused, proceeded to hold his lesson as though nothing had been said: 'Tropes encompass the metaphor, synecdoche, metonymy, antonomasia, onomatopoeia, catachresis and metalepsis. *Allegoria nihil alius est quam continua Metaphora . . .*'

At this point Madam Rastina placed her fan on Papila's lips, stroked him with her silvery eyes and quietly continued to speak: 'Be it in a metaphor or allegory, it is all the same, the woman of the story one day in horror called her husband over to listen: in the back of the armchair one could hear a heart beating . . .'

'*Dic quibus interris et eris mihi magnus Apollo* . . .'

'A month or two later, the outline of a curled embryo was quite visible under the slipcover, and when someone leaned back, the child inside would nestle up, in search of warmth and the beating of another's heart. Soon, by slightly lifting the slipcover, one could see that the child was a boy . . .'

'*Crudelis Mater magis, an puer imquebus ille*
Improbus ille puer, crudelis tu quaque Mater . . .'

With these words, and with horror in his soul, the distraught Avksentije endeavoured to continue his futile lesson, but suddenly Madam Rastina finished her story:

'Finally the back of the chair was ripped open and inside they found you, Avksentije Papila!'

As these words were spoken Avksentije shook from head to foot, screamed and threw himself into the open arms of Madam Rastina, who shielded him from his terrible thoughts by clutching him to her breast and taking him from the armchair of the story straight to her bed.

During these days of 1813 in Karlovci, the moonlight wore a green lining, a wind swept away not hats but names, and a greasy, nourishing rain fell.

'Look at them,' prattled Madam Rastina, pointing to the ladies passing by in the wind, as she looked out of her window which resembled a floating glass sedan chair. 'Look at them, each holds her name between her breasts. The first to slip his hand in there will carry away their name. But, above all, beware of those who are good-looking,' Mrs Kaloperović said during those days to her son and to her lover, delighted by the sudden return of youth. 'Beware of those whose upper lip is green and lower lip is purple. Of those on whose earrings birds alight. They will give you water to drink from the cup of their hand, water in which sage spent the night, water which makes one forget one's own mother.'

As she spoke, her son Aleksa gazed at her, his mother, no longer recognizing her, and she gazed at Papila as though he were an angel.

During those weeks, the taste of mushroom juice, which she liked, changed in Madam Rastina's mouth, cinnamon acquired the taste of coffee and Mrs Kaloperović, who had already heard her wooden horse on the shore of night and the darkness on the shore of names, was transfigured.

'Can you come to me in my dreams for once?' she asked her lover. 'I never seem able to arrange it so that I fuck you, Papila, in my dreams as well. And I can no longer dream about Arsenije.'

On one of the following mornings she said to him, 'You scared the daylights out of me in my dream last night. You crept in with a lantern. I called you into my dream to caress me, but you wanted to kill me. And with a Hussar's sabre, too!'

To calm her down, the young Papila bestowed on her his smile which, the ladies of Karlovci whispered, was 'worth a riding horse' and a blue pillow with a bell on each of its four ears; so that she would remember him even when she slept. Written across the pillow in gold thread in Latin was the following:

*When Madam Rastina lies down, the bells jingle and
dreams drop out of them. When Madam Rastina gets up,
the dreams go back into the bells, and Madam Rastina's cat
crawls into the bed. It purrs and paws at the little bells.
When one of Madam Rastina's dreams falls out of the bell,
the cat opens its mouth and swallows it. But the food is too
strong and does not agree with the cat. Then the cat becomes
afraid of what it has swallowed and stops purring for a few
days, looking for real hyssop, which it uses against snake-
bite. With the help of this herb it too recovers from Madam
Rastina's dream.*

On the other side of the pillow was written: 'The name
of the cat is Avksentije Papila.'

Madam Rastina proudly carried this pillow to her
window, gazed at Papila adoringly with her silvery
eyes, for love of him learned again how to walk with a
burning candle in a candlestick on the crown of her
head and, after many long years, took her clarinet out
of the black nacre and velvet box. One afternoon, her
face slightly flushed, she played for her son and her
lover Haydn's *Divertimento – Corale di Sant'Antonio – per
lauto, oboe, clarinetto, fagotto e corno* and just as she
reached the 'Minuetto' into the room walked her
daughter Dunja with her upper lip painted green and
lower lip painted yellow.

Madam Rastina choked, stopped playing and that
same evening secretly tossed a goat's hide over her
daughter's bed. The next day she examined her lover
and on Avksentije's back noticed scratches from the
coarse goat hair. Driven mad with fear, that night she
waited until she saw her daughter wash herself.
Watching her through the curtain, Madam Rastina

thought for an instant how a man will never know how a woman washing herself feels, nor will a woman ever know how a man shaking himself off after urinating feels . . . It was then that she noticed on Dunja's knees the reddish streaks from the goat's hair. And so she learned more than she had wanted to know.

She passed the night in helpless fury, she could have walked to Slankamen with all her pacing up and down the room. In the morning she summoned her son, embraced him and told him everything. The two were weeping in each other's arms when suddenly he pulled away, went into the room where Papila was giving his sister her Latin lesson and, aiming his pistols, drove them both out of the house.

The Chariot

FOR a while, nothing was heard of Dunja and Papila, except that old Mr Kaloperović was secretly supporting them without his wife's knowledge. But soon one of those terrible stories connected with Avksentije Papila again reached Madam Rastina's ears.

After the lovers had been banished from the Kaloperović house, Papila continued for a while to help the sexton in the Karlovci upper church keep the birth and death records. At a certain moment, however, Papila was caught filling in, next to the births column, the deaths column for those very same newly born and registered infants, giving the exact day, month and year of these still unchristened children's future deaths. Although all the death columns were erased as soon as Avksentije Papila's wrongdoing was discovered, the horrified parents could not forget the dates recorded in Papila's hand under the still remote years that were far into the eighteen hundreds.

Matters did not end there. When a child died of measles and the date in the records of the upper church in Karlovci was compared with the actual date of death, it transpired that Papila had recorded the year and the day correctly and that there was nothing new to inscribe. Some parents then insisted on seeing the books, wanting to check the fate of their children against the crossed-out columns. Finally, an investigation was conducted *in situ*. The sheriff brought Papila along, who was no longer allowed into the school, to show what he had done with the birth and death records. When the books were opened in front of him, Papila instantly found the place where his own birth had been recorded, grabbed the pen from the sexton's hand, dipped it in his mouth and wrote in the date of his own death.

Condemned to leave Karlovci, Dunja and Papila set out to see the world. Papila signed up with the Austrian army and Dunja went to see him off to fight the French. On the way she thought fearfully of the date Papila had inscribed next to his name in the births and deaths register of the upper church in Karlovci; of the date which had been immediately erased from the books and which Papila would not reveal to anyone. Whenever she asked him about the date, he would reply, 'You kill a fish with a rock like felling a bird in the sky with a snowball, then you make a soup and find the fish's name at the bottom of it. That name is not for eating and not for publication.'

But he himself, of course, knew the date. The date of Papila's death was in the second half of the century and it promised him a long life.

Astonishing stories followed Avksentije Papila even in the battlefield. According to one, Avksentije, together with his superior, Captain Pana Tenecki, the son of the famous Pahomije Tenecki, went to see a play by a travelling theatre. They were performing *The Three Deaths of Captain Opujić*. After the show Avksentije thought to himself: Why, that Captain Opujić is this same Captain Opujić whose French unit we are pursuing. The same one who killed the father of my Captain Pana Tenecki in the last war. And Captain Pana is playing dumb. Maybe he is testing me.

And then it suddenly dawned on him. Captain Opujić's third and final death had not yet occurred! In other words, the captain could still be killed. He had only three lives and if someone were to take from him his third life, like the ninth life of a cat, it would be the end of his reign in the battlefield. Avksentije procured a lantern and resolved to seek out Captain Opujić in his next battle.

'I shall strip him of his stirrups,' said Papila, who had already demonstrated his prowess in the battle-field. He played 'the rabbit'; he would charge into battle first, with the others in tow, and then would drop back to the rear and wait for the next opportunity. He was waiting for an opportunity now. And it was afforded him in a town. Second Lieutenant Papila's Austrian unit stopped at a small stone square as silent as a room. Right in the middle of it stood a building which, he was told, was a university. Papila was astounded to see that all the walls of the building were waist-high with liberal amounts of pee. The urine had dried long ago, but clearly many people had participated in the act. The students had obviously peed on their university. On one wall live coal had been used to write in large bold letters:

ICH HATTE SCHLECHTE LEHRER,
DAS WAR EINE GUTE SCHULE

Behind this inscription, inside the university building, was the French unit they had been pursuing.

That same night, in a side street off the square, Captain Opujić, who was making the rounds of his guards, and Second Lieutenant Papila, who with a foolish display of courage had stepped out in front of him, came face to face. For a moment both were in no man's land, both held lanterns and sabres in their hands. Papila did not indulge in military calculations. He relied on the stage play in which this was exactly how Opujić's third death began. Papila stuck his sabre into the ground, hung the lantern on it and retreated into the darkness with his knife in hand. And the captain did the same at his own end of the street, Papila assumed, meaning that he too had stuck his sabre into the ground and on it hung his lantern. The young man expected Opujić to retreat into the darkness as well, where he, Papila, would be waiting for him with his ready knife. At one moment Papila even swung around at the sound of something behind him, slashing the air with his knife, but no one was there. A black butterfly looking like two keys on a ring, simply brushed his cheek with its wing. In short, Papila found not a soul in the darkness. He searched and he searched, but Captain Opujić was nowhere to be found. The second lieutenant had already begun to think that someone was pulling his leg. Angry and wet after his futile search in the dark and mud, he headed straight for his opponent's lantern and sabre to claim them as war booty. But just as that booty was within arm's reach, the captain, who had not moved from his sabre and lantern, doused the flame and in the ensuing darkness smote him so hard with his sabre that Papila's tongue fell out of his ear. Opujić went his way, while Avksentije Papila lay in the street in the mud, no longer young. Because the dead are never young.

The news of Avksentije's death reached Sremski Karlovci by water. The first to hear it was Master Jeremije Kaloperović. One of Karlovci's jokesters, the kind who rests on one shadow and covers himself with another, entered Jeremije's shop and related the following:

'I heard a nice little story down by the pier today. Two peasants had sold their oxen, collected quite a bit of money and were returning home. And the French were retreating through Prussia; with them so were the Serbs who served Bonaparte. To pass the hours one of the peasants wagered a hundred coins that he could eat a frog. And our Serbs in the Austrian army were attacking the French passing through German land; and with them so was Papila, our Avksentije Papila of the upper church. The peasant really did eat the frog and claimed his money. And Papila challenged a French captain Opujić to a duel, one of the Opujićes from over there in Trieste. And the peasant who lost the bet over the frog and had to pay out a hundred coins thought to himself: The village will laugh at me when they hear what I paid for. And your Dunja was no longer with our men, with the Austrians, because that particular Captain Opujić had sent her off to heal the wounds of his injured son, Sofronije, a lieutenant in the French army. So the other peasant, hoping to recoup his one hundred coins, wagered that he too could eat a frog! And he did. And Captain Opujić killed Papila with his sabre, without even asking his name, while the peasant who had eaten the frog asked the first peasant, after getting back his hundred coins:

'Tell me, why did we Serbs swallow these frogs?'

Master Kaloperović chased the miscreant out of his shop, but for the rest of the day he did not dare appear before his wife with the dreadful news. He hid his tears, but the news quickly spread and Madam Rastina, who was inseparable from her now tear-soaked pillow with its bells, heard the news of Papila's death after her husband, although she had heard another terrible story before him, one of those tales which swarmed around Papila even in death.

Sitting on the veranda overlooking the Danube that afternoon were Madam Rastina and her friend Mrs Avakumović, who had come for the express purpose of telling her immediately all about it.

'When Avksentije Papila was killed,' said Mrs Avakumović, 'your Dunja took a fish-shaped knife and disappeared to avenge her lover. She went looking for the person who had killed him, and it was known who that was – old Captain Opujić. She found her lover's killer in a French bivouac and the soldiers brought her in to him.

'I have come from afar to seek your hand. I have heard it is exceptionally light and swift with a sabre. That is why I need you. I have a request.'

'What request?' asked Captain Opujić.

'I need someone removed.'

'That takes money.'

'Of course it does,' said Dunja, showing him a pouch of gold.

'All right,' he said, 'who is it who needs to be removed?'

'Me.'

'You? You are paying to have yourself killed?'

'That's right. And I have no time to lose. I am in a hurry. I have just one condition. You see this slightly grey hair of mine? When you do your job it must stay as it is. Not a single little moon, not a single little star of grey must be damaged.'

Suddenly he pulled a bridle over her head and shoved the bit between her teeth. The soldiers were appalled, but the headstall fitted surprisingly well and the bit found its niche between the teeth as though it had all been made for Dunja's own head.

'Now we know where we stand. Fleas do not go on fat cats,' the captain added, swinging his scabbard upside down and letting the huge sabre fall out. He held out the scabbard to Dunja and she filled it with gold coins. Then he unbridled her and ordered them to bring out the round butter breads which take all day to bake, because each is removed from the oven as soon as the next one is kneaded and buttered, and then the new one is added to the old and they are returned to the oven all together. After dinner he led Dunja to the bed chamber, saying, 'Surely you are not afraid to lie down with someone of whom you seek the kind of service you ask of me?'

'I am not afraid of anything any more,' Dunja replied, 'but tell me what you are going to do to me. They say you are unpredictable in your actions . . .' And she glanced at the sky as if measuring time.

'I shall give you the most beautiful death known to womankind. Inside me are the seed of death and the seed of life. I shall make you a child and you will give birth to whichever you wish. You will be doubly impregnated and decide for yourself which of the two seeds you want: the seed of life or the seed of death.'

'That will take too long. I want it done right now.'

'It won't take long, it will be done this very night.'

Dunja embraced her executioner and felt the night inside her split open, leaving room for a sweet light. And then everything fell silent. And she did not use her hidden knife. The knife shaped like a fish.

'Now you can stay with me,' he said in the morning, kissing her on the ring. Dunja realized that she would live and probably was glad.

'Your seed did not kill me,' she said.

'No, it did not, but it did not impregnate you either. You are childless.' And they both laughed . . .

This was the story that the appalled Madam Rastina heard from her friend. That evening she paced up and down her room again and, furious with her daughter, kept repeating deliriously: 'She has no cunt! She has no cunt! To lose Papila. A man like that! And not to use her knife!'

But at dinner that evening her husband told her that their Arsenije had enlisted in the army, determined to avenge his friend Papila, to kill Opujić and seize his sister. That frightened Madam Rastina even more and, summoning her son, she said through her tears:

'Now we both have chains around our necks. But they are not tight, we can cast them off if we want and continue as though nothing had happened. Do you want to?'

'Of course not,' replied the young Kaloperović, already in Hussar dress.

'Then swear to me that you will sleep with every woman Papila bedded.'

Seeing the strange light that flashed in her son's eyes as she uttered these words, Madam Rastina seemed to perk up. She made her son swear that he would sleep with every woman bedded by his late friend Avksentije Papila and thus preserve Avksentije's memory and, in a way, keep him alive through the women who had loved him. And she swore to herself that she would seize back her daughter and rival, who had deprived her of Avksentije for ever, and of all the people her daughter had slept with or would want to sleep with.

'And one more thing,' she whispered into her son's ear as he leaned down from his saddle to kiss her before going off to fight the French:

'You know, I did not dare tell you before. But now I must. Captain Opujić is your father.'

The young Arsenije Kaloperović jumped at these words. He felt grass growing on his tongue. Instead of revenge, he saw ahead of him several quick, short affairs with women who had once been his friend's loves and who would now have to be his as well.

At the time when he decided to mix his own seed

with that of his dead friend, Arsenije did not yet realize the full meaning of his promise. He merely
thought that in the light of his new knowledge, Dunja
was not his sister but his half-sister.

And he happily spurred on his horse.

The Second Seven Keys

KEY 8

STRENGTH

JERISENA Tenecki could not remember her father, who had died in 1797 in a tower on the Danube, but in thinking of him she learned to fly. First, she flew in her dreams. Later, she even flew around her room a little. Jerisena Tenecki looked out of her window in Zemun at the waters of the Danube, at night she noticed how the smells of these waters changed and by day how the waves cast shadows on the shore. Her father was buried somewhere in those waters and she, who had especially loved her father because he had lost battles in war, would sometimes whisper to the great waters, 'Play with him, you devils, but then return him to me.'

But her father did not return. That morning she

suddenly came tearing out of the room where she was cold from the armoire and where it never stopped raining in her dreams. She carried her breasts down the stairs to the river as if they were not her own; they surprised her, she listened to her still unfamiliar body, as though condemned to the multicoloured liquid inside her. And she felt that she had to populate that body. That it was desolate. That the emptiness inside it hurt. That youth was a sin and a punishment. There, on the stairs, she hated her handsome older brother, Captain Pana Tenecki of the Austrian army, who had just returned from Trieste with an untameable lion's mane over his shoulders. She hated him as much as those around her feared him, and down by the dockyard shacks she hated her younger brother Makarije Tenecki, who, before getting married, had made locks and handles in the family bell foundry which were as exact as clocks and, after he married, began making in that same bell foundry hammers and triggers on pistols and muskets, just as perfect, for the Austrian army. In front of the Church of St Nicholas she hated her long and narrow feet, which she thought were ugly, and at the end of the road, by the fountain, she hated Makarije's wife who had said of her: 'Jerisena Tenecki, you can neither push nor pull.' For a while, the hate inside her wrestled with an opposite force, but then she began to cry and that helped her to dispel it.

I know what I will use against this hate inside me, she thought and down on the shore, which was as clean and swept as a room, she entered a shop and picked out several things to buy.

'Give me that kerchief, a chibouk, this chair, a pair

of gloves and a ring.'

'That is no way to buy things, Miss Tenecki,' the shopkeeper advised. 'You must tell me what kind of chibouk you want. There are men's pipes and women's. Meerschaum and those that keep burning when you lay them aside. And there are others which fit the hand that will hold them, carved to measure.'

'I don't have the measurements yet,' replied Jerisena, thinking that her tears had betrayed her. She felt as though her thoughts showed on her face, as though thoughts and dreams could be read in one's tears.

Tears betray you even when they are dry, Jerisena thought, when they can no longer be distinguished from yesterday's sweat and when they lie on the cheek like fish scales.

Still, as if she were choosing an instrument she picked out a hard pipe made of the wood of a plum tree, its mouthpiece made of horn.

'As for the gloves, give me a pair of men's gloves. The kind you wear a ring over. And give me a ring to go with them.'

The shopkeeper muttered that it would be better to make the gloves to size and to fit the ring to the finger, but Jerisena said she knew the size of the person she was buying it for. That was not true. The person she was buying it for was completely unknown to her at the time. She did not even know what he looked like or what his name was. She had never seen him. Jerisena Tenecki was buying things for her as yet unknown intended, for her future husband, who would certainly surface one day from the open sea of the future, on which daily flowed the waters of this

Danube that lay at her feet and at the foot of the town. She bought everything at once, as if it were for her trousseau. Paying for the ring, her whole body began to smell of peaches.

From one of the displays on the steps she removed a pair of tiny silver and silk shoes, hanging from a gold ribbon.

'Will you sell me one of these little shoes?' she asked the shopkeeper.

'One?' asked the shopkeeper, feeling that he was rapidly growing a beard, like a dead man. 'Who has ever heard of buying just one shoe, dear child?'

With a dismissive wave of her hand Jerisena Tenecki paid for the pair of shoes and immediately tossed one into the ditch and hung the other around her neck like a locket. And so, with the little shoe glistening like a precious jewel between her breasts, she returned home. That evening, as soon as her purchases were delivered, she distributed them around the room and gave them names. She called the ring her 'Hound' and only then did she notice that it had an inscription:

Remember me! The ring is virginity renewed. I await your finger as your bridegroom!

She dropped it into her third shoe and dozed off. When the nearby Church of St Nicholas struck the hour of midnight, she felt in her sleep how her body was beginning to smell of peaches again. And the smell frightened her.

In fact, Jerisena Tenecki did not like to sleep. She was afraid of falling asleep.

KEY 9

$\mathscr{T}$HE $\mathscr{H}$ERMIT

LIEUTENANT Sofronije Opujić of the French army rode his horse barefoot, like someone who had stuck a gold coin into a loaf of bread and then let the bread drift downstream. He let the soldiers rest on the slope of a hill and went alone to the hut at the top, where a hermit was trying to chop wood. A word from Opujić and the soldiers came to the aid of the recluse. Returning from their mission that night, they plunged into such darkness that they had to stop. And then on the hill a lantern flashed. The hermit was lighting their way in return for the fire they had given him. The lieutenant ordered movement, but as he spoke the light went out. As soon as he stopped talking, the light came back on again. The lieutenant ordered the men to be silent, but at that moment a horse neighed and the light vanished in the mists of darkness.

Who will give us a giver whose gifts do not die with him, when even the stars fall off their light like leaves? thought Sofronije and ordered the men to hold the horses' mouths shut. And that is how they managed to tackle the hill.

Opujić ordered the men to spend the night there and knocked on the door of the hut. The hermit let him in and gave him a corner to lie down in. They lay there in the dark and Sofronije said not a word. The hermit was one of those who could tell the day of the year from the leap of a chamois or tomorrow's weather from the sound of the water.

And the lieutenant felt that small pang of hunger awaken inside him like a pain under the heart and through the hunger and pain he listened to the roar of the subterranean rivers and waters deep down under the earth as they twisted and turned in their depths or spilled on to the metallic pebbles and silvery sand. He heard how the waters carried the underground fish to the north and how the desire at the bottom of his soul responded to these movements and sounds, to this music and its vibration and he knew that all this in the womb of the earth was merely the reverberation of the trembling of the stars and that this was how gold in the earth spoke with gold in the universe, and with animals, plants and the ancestors in man. He yearned for everything about him to change as much as possible. He had absolutely no reason to like his past, but he did have hopes of the future and loved it, even though it led him toward death. Everything lay ahead of him, nothing behind him. He was driven and carried by the desire and hope that a miracle might happen, that the distribution of the planets above might change, that time, which beat like a second heart in his pocket, would stop striking off the hours to his detriment, that Aquarius and Scorpio would hire themselves out to some other service and that the hermit would then be unable to tell from the leap of the chamois the hour on Lieutenant Sofronije Opujić's watch. Thanks to this non-corporeal desire, he glowed with a kind of light, not an ordinary light but a strange one which could be taken into the mouth like water. But that light was not of this world and could not lead him through the night; it could lead him only through the underworld. And it was from the terrestrial world that he needed some light.

'I know why you are not sleeping,' the hermit then said. 'You are going into battle soon. You came for me to tell you what is going to happen in that battle . . .'

Lieutenant Opujić said nothing and listened, because he already knew from experience that the light would not be given to him if he spoke.

'Well, this is how things stand with you, my son. Think of two numbers – one male and one female. Or, better and easier still, think of two enemy armies in battle. One wins, as did the French army in the last war, where your father was. The other loses, as did the Austrian army. But beware – victory has no children, it has only a father. Whereas defeat has a hundred children. Think about it. Who is the stronger? And after the victory what happens to the victors? A terrible, bearded and, to you, unknown man, armed to the teeth, covered in mud from head to foot, suddenly burst into the house, frightened you to death with his unfamiliar smell and bedded your mother before you managed to get out of the room and realize that this was your father. And the same thing happened in every victor's home. Thereafter they kept, and still keep, a tight rein on their women, their horses and their power. As for their children – you and your generation – they will keep you in their shadow and on a leash until you start to count your grey hairs.

'But now look at that other enemy tunic, in the backyard of the neighbouring state that lost the war to your father and the French. There, fathers, brought to their knees, returned home with their tails between their legs. The army of defeated fathers swept their whole country with misery. The whole of Austria and Prussia. And what happened? Their sons, your peers, who did not carry arms at the time, did not carry guilt for the lost war. They had no sins on their soul, no barriers ahead of them, no fathers riding their backs. That is why today they can do all the things you never dared to do. The can do all the things your fathers could do. You want proof? The proof lies on your shoulder. In the last war your father Haralampije Opujić killed a famous Austrian gunner, Pahomije Tenecki. And now, after all those years, you, the son of your victorious father, together with the son of the defeated Pahomije Tenecki, are soldiers yourselves. But remember, you in Napoleon's and he in the Austrian army do not have the same rank. You are a lieutenant and he, albeit your peer, has already made captain, which means that the generation of the powerful in that neighbouring army which lost the last war to your fathers, is a generation younger than that of the powerful in your army, where your doddering fathers still rule. But now you, the weak, face them, the powerful on the other side of the target sight, you who have no rights even today but will bear all the responsibility and risk in this new showdown. The weak generation of the one-time victors' sons will clash in this war with the omnipotent generation of the losers' sons. So beware and remember that this is a very challenging time for you . . .

'But there is something I want to ask, something I do not understand about you and your father. I do not understand it even about your enemy, Captain Tenecki. Why are you serving in foreign armies rather than in your own? You are fighting and dying for two foreign empires, for France and for Austria, and all the while your fellow tribesmen in Serbia and in Belgrade are fighting for their country against the Turks.'

While the hermit talked, the officer standing next to him in the dark heard how in the dizzying depths beneath the hermit's hut, mists of different colours – red, yellow, green and blue – were flying about in the darkness, like the winds blowing overhead. And he stopped thinking about the battle awaiting him. It was that hour of the night when moustaches grow more quickly and he felt something like a cobweb tickling his lips.

'What is the right path, Father?' he asked finally. 'How does one recognize it?'

'If you follow the direction of your fear, you will be on the right path. And may God help you.'

THE WHEEL OF FORTUNE

ONE evening a young woman appeared in lieutenant Opujić's camp. They brought her to him in the house he had requisitioned. Her black hair was sprinkled with grey in the shape of little stars and crescents, like white flowers.

'Is that silver powder?' the young Opujić wondered, and the girl said, 'Your father, Captain Opujić, sent me, sir, to convey his greetings and to give you a ring.'

'What kind of ring?' asked the young Opujić .

The girl said nothing.

'Have you got the night in your mouth?' he asked. She then said shyly, 'Your father heard that you had been wounded in the shoulder.'

'What has that got to do with you?'

'I am a healer. Your father sent me to lick your wounds so that some bitch doesn't lick you, he says. And he sent the ring for you to give to me for my efforts.' She held out the signet ring with what the lieutenant recognized to be his father's initials.

'What is your name?' he asked her.

'I am Dunja Kaloperović of Karlovci, on the Danube,' replied the girl.

The officer lay himself down and Dunja took a drop of brandy and made the sign of the cross over his wound. But before she got down to work she warned him:

'Look at my hair. When the wound heals, you may find that instead of proud flesh, it grows something like hair, something like a black hairy wing made of my hair. You can keep clipping it, but it will sprout like a beard. Is that all right?'

The young Opujić simply gave a dismissive wave of his hand. As she licked his injuries, he lay still on his back and through the glassy night listened to the tumultuous roar of the waters underneath the earth, as if there, in the womb of the earth, storms were raging. Ever since that incomprehensible desire had taken hold of him, Lieutenant Opujić's hearing had become receptive to secret things, he heard the underground better than others did the above-ground. Sitting in his heart above the night he chased the cry of the buried waters, the explosion of the lakes which deep down below extinguished the dormant volcanoes by spilling on to their fire. And he listened to the respiration of the subterranean rivers and to how they responded to the breathing of the moon, carrying their ebb and flow through the womb of the earth . . . And to how his own wound, his hunger and his pain responded and throbbed to the rhythm of the pulse beating underground.

When Dunja finished, she crossed herself and said, as if accidentally catching sight of his erect eleventh finger:

'For a while you should pee sitting down . . .'

And she laughed into her moonlit sleeve. He inquired then about his father and she replied that Captain Opujić was well. And again she laughed into her sleeve.

'Why are you laughing?' asked the lieutenant and Dunja told him. On her way here she had heard that a group of magicians, fortune-tellers, healers and actors had a camp near by where they staged some kind of plays about the lieutenant's father, Captain Haralampije Opujić.

'About his love life. One sad play is called *Last Love in Constantinople*,' she whispered. 'I saw it in Segedin. And I cried. He disappears from this life because of his last love, because a woman in Constantinople had fallen in love with him and had wanted to have his child . . .'

As soon as Dunja had gone to her room, the young Opujić took a sip of his wine and, with a perfect shot from his mouth, doused the candle in the window without ever leaving his bed.

When Lieutenant Sofronije's wound began to heal, he gave Dunja his father's ring, which meant that it was time for them to part. But, laughing into her sleeve, she said that now something else needed healing, not the wound.

'And what would that be?' he asked, pinching her cheek.

'It is not healthy for this male organ of yours to be

standing up straight all the time. I would love to know how old it is. Doesn't it collapse even after making love?'

'No.'

'I have something to confess to you, sir. Your father did not send me to heal you. He does not even know that you are wounded. And I haven't a clue about healing. I am not a healer at all.'

'Why did he send you then?'

'He says I have good breasts. That's why. And his message is that he will send you another girl my age if she proves worthy.'

'And you are telling me this only now?'

'You were a wounded man until now.'

'How many girls your age does he have?'

'All girls my age are mad about him.'

'What does he do with you?'

'He is like a father to us. With him we are not afraid. Plus he keeps amusing and surprising us. And I am hard to surprise.'

'How did he surprise you?'

'Never mind. I have long wanted to see how you will surprise me.'

The lieutenant laughed at her words and asked, 'What is the name of that foreign pleasure between your legs?'

'Jevdokija.'

'Well then, let us give Jevdokija a treat. Tell me, what is Jevdokija's favourite food?

Dunja whispered something into his ear and Sofronije ordered a sumptuous dinner for three. And he ordered the dining table, damask, silverware and crystal which had been brought in with all the delicacies and drinks to be laid out on the bed. Then he and

Dunja stretched out on the couch and he gave Jevdokija a spoonful of cauliflower soup to drink, some creamed mushrooms to taste, a bit of pilaff, a little radish, a chicken leg, which she nibbled clean tossing away the bone, and lastly he fed her a grape. When he saw that Jevdokija was full, he embraced Dunja and said, 'Let's wash down dinner!'

After they had made love, she remained in bed and Sofronije threw his army coat over his shoulders, unsealed his papers and writing box and sat down to write a letter home:

And write and tell me how things are with you this year – will there be any hay and wheat, are the vineyards beautiful and bearing fruit, and what else is happening? You write nothing, dear brothers Marko and Lukijan, about whether you are selling anything or not, about whether the cattle is healthy and all in one piece . . . We here keep waiting every second and we pray to God for the good Lord to give to our bodily eyes the power to see you again!

I send greetings to my dear, sweet sisters Jovana and Sara and to my dear, good sisters-in-law Marta and Anica; let them not worry about me, but rather be thoughtful of each other and live in harmony and let them obey and respect my mother Paraskeva, and may the good Lord grace them with every treasure He holds dear . . .

Written on the day of the Holy Apostle Jeremiah, the last in our month of May, and theirs of June, your son and brother in dreams
    Sofronije

⑦USTICE

𝒞APTAIN Pana Tenecki of the Austrian army and three men from his detachment walked into 'The Man's' barbershop and ordered a trim and a plate of roast duckling fattened on cheese. Standing in the middle of the barbershop was 'the man' – a wooden statue of a man pouring water. The boys flurried around the officers, trimmed their hair and offered them brandy and candied flowers – violets and roses. Then they laid a table for them right there in the middle of the barbershop and the officers dined. To the astonishment of the wig-maker, the barber and the boys, after lunch Captain Tenecki, the towel still tucked under his chin, returned to the barber's chair and ordered his and his companions' heads shaved clean. And their eyebrows removed.

'Why do that, Captain?' said the barber finding the courage to speak. 'Hair is like clothing.'

'Precisely,' said Tenecki settling into the chair. 'Ugly men fight better.'

While their heads were being shaved, he instructed his orderly, who was waiting for him at the door, to have his sabre sharpened for his left hand. And the scabbard as well.

'The captain surely means the sabre, not the scabbard.'

'My sabre is always sharp, little man, now you stick your tail in your mouth and listen!' he replied to the orderly, who disappeared to sharpen the scabbard and the sabre for the left hand, somewhat surprised because he knew the captain was right-handed.

'Are you preparing for a fresh victory, mein Herr?' asked the barber, cutting the captain's hair for the second time.

'Wrong, my eagle, I am preparing to stay where I am.'

'Which is to say, mein Herr?'

'Have you ever seen a fresco of Christ giving Communion?'

'Christ? Yes, I have, there are two of them: one gives out bread and the other wine. One always faces one side of the world, and the other faces the other side.'

'Correct. You see how quickly you understood that? Since bread and wine cannot be given at the same time, it means that the Christ giving the bread is older than the Christ giving the wine, or vice versa. In other words, the moment that wine is the future, bread is the past. And so it is with the sides of the world. Painted on the fresco of the communion of the apostles, therefore, is time.'

'And where are you, captain?'

'I am always in between. In between two Christs, in between east and west, in between bread and wine, or if you like in between the past and the future. And that is where I wish to remain. Something my late father failed to do. Indeed he was no soldier. He was a musician and he thought only in terms of pauses. He did not know that life depends on enemies, not on friends.'

'Well, yes, you Serbs pay more attention to your enemies than to your friends. Well done, captain. It is said that on the opposing French side is Lieutenant Sofronije Opujić. Of the famous Opujićes of Trieste. Beware of him. He too, they say, is like his father. As fast as a tooth. Just in case, position one of your men with a gun in a blanket between two horses. And have him keep an eye on the lieutenant.'

'He is no famous Opujić. He still pisses in his daddy's shadow,' interrupted one of the officers.

'In any event, he is an odd one. He dropped in here the other day.'

'You don't say? Really?' one of the officers said.

'I swear on this cross, he dropped in with an unusual order. He mentioned you, Captain Tenecki, by name. He said his father knew your father.'

'The finger has found the pie,' cut in Captain Tenecki. 'It is important to have a father only once in your life. And you know when that is. After that you do not need him. As for Lieutenant Opujić, I used to know his sister Jovana well, but I do not know her any more.'

'What is there to say, mein Herr? There is no choice, people see the devil and the devil sees God.'

'And what was it that Opujić ordered?' the officer in the third chair wanted to know.

'He ordered a trim and a shave after death, "just in case", should the worst happen. They say he always orders that before any battle. And he pays in advance. The Opujićes want to look good even in death.'

'And so they shall,' Captain Tenecki cut in. He threw off the towel and strode out into the sunlight, where his shaved pate glistened.

'What is going on?' one shop boy asked the other, after the officers had left.

'Don't you get it?' said the other.

'No.'

'Captain Pana Tenecki is seeking justice. Here in this war, in 1813, he wants to take his revenge on Lieutenant Sofronije Opujić, the son of Captain Haralampije Opujić who, in the last war, in 1797, killed his father Pahomije Tenecki.'

Three days later Sofronije and Pana did indeed meet on the battlefront. With their heads and eyebrows shaven clean, Pana Tenecki and his officers looked like ghosts. For this occasion Captain Tenecki switched his sabre to his left hand, holding the scabbard in his right. When they charged at each other Lieutenant Sofronije Opujić thought that his opponent was left-handed and so kept his eye on the sabre in Tenecki's left hand . . . That was when Tenecki stabbed him with the scabbard in his right hand and the young Opujić fell as if cut down. The last thing he saw as he lay there stabbed was Captain Pana Tenecki signalling victory and the end of the battle by returning his sabre to its scabbard without removing the latter from Opujić's chest. And the sabre slid wondrously and easily into the scabbard and Sofronije's body, causing no pain.

$\mathscr{T}$HE $\mathscr{H}$ANGED $\mathscr{M}$AN

$\mathscr{L}$EAVING the scene of his victory, Captain Pana Tenecki ordered Lieutenant Sofronije Opujić to be suspended from a tree by one foot. The lieutenant was thus left to hang upside-down, his hands tied behind his back. His beautiful long hair fell down and for the first time in many years he was unable to hear a single sound either below ground or above.

That night, however, a girl with a shoe hanging around her neck arrived on the scene and found the hanged man. She looked at him carefully, saw that his male organ was standing straight, deduced therefore that he was alive and immediately ordered her servants to untie the lieutenant and take him to a house in the nearby town. The Austrian soldiers in Captain

Tenecki's unit did not stand in her way; on the contrary, they seemed to be slightly afraid of her.

In town, Sofronije was stripped naked and put to bed in fresh, clean sheets. In the process, the girl discovered on his shoulder a lock of raven-black hair with tiny star- and crescent-shaped flecks of grey in it and hanging from his belt a pouch containing a gold bracelet. Like all young girls, she thought the most important thing was what was inscribed in the mirror, but she gladly read what was inscribed on the bracelet as well. She then slipped the bracelet on her hand, had a sense of satisfaction and set about cleaning the lieutenant's wound. Strangely enough, like his white imperial hounds, the young man had no smell and, like them, he did not get soiled, his body being capable of cleaning itself. But in this case that was not of much help. Sofronije Opujić was in a hopeless condition and the girl realized that she had to act quickly, very quickly.

She was not afraid of what she had to do. She listened carefully to the injured man's breathing and seized on the moment that he released the air from his lungs. That same instant she inhaled deeply, sucking the pain out of him, trying to take upon herself the energies of evil emanating from his body. And then, when Sofronije inhaled, she exhaled, transmitting to the sick man the healthy energies of her young body. Thus proceeded the removal of these harmful energies which, because the girl was not afraid of her action, were carried off into the wind. But she was soon exhausted by this cure and, she noticed, so was he, just as childbirth exhausts both mother and child. She therefore interrupted the treatment, and the lieutenant thought he heard something deep down inside him.

First he heard the windows in the wardrobes of the spacious room where he was lying. Then, ten fathoms under his bed he heard rock cracking at the bottom of a fissure and felt that the human soul had its east, its west, its south and its north. And somehow he knew that he was at the north of his soul. It was cold and he listened for a wind from the south, and when he actually heard it he turned slowly in that direction and moved through the night to the south. To the south of his soul. And during that journey, which took days and weeks, a strange thing was revealed and explained to the lieutenant.

Man – Opujić realized, rocking in the wooden bed as if it were a boat, with a canopy in lieu of sails – man had lived for thousands of years without noticing that in nature all around him there were numbers. Billions of numbers. Then one morning, quite by chance, man noticed his first number, like a flower in the grass. Like a first smile. Just as he had difficulty in discovering his tomorrow, so it was with difficulty that he discovered his first number. It took him another few thousand years to get to the next number, indeed longer than it had taken him to discover his day-after-tomorrow. Finally he began to tame and domesticate the numbers around him. To breed them. And under his touch and eye they flourished. But only for him. The numbers existed for no one else on earth, below earth or above earth. Not for the animals, not for the plants. At first he thought that the dead forgot numbers, but then, gazing into the water, he saw the stars and realized that there were numbers in heaven as well, in infinite quantity. Just as his ancestor Adam had given names to the animals, so man started to give names to these innumerable numbers. But the numbers were so many that everything came to a halt within Sofronije's soul. Just when the taming of the celestial numbers should have started in his hearing, Sofronije had not a drop of strength left.

Suddenly he was in the upper north-western corner of the room and saw himself lying naked in bed, his hair spilling over the pillow. That hair had streaks of grey which he did not immediately recognize and which obviously grew more slowly than the raven-black hair on his head, as a result of which all the grey locks were shorter. His chest was encased in a bird-cage without a top and without a bottom and he was wedged inside it and had to lie there without moving. Although he could see all this from his own corner, it was not Lieutenant Opujić but his shirt, his boots and his bicorn hat that had been duplicated. That was when he started to die and the first thing he lost was his sex, then he felt his shirt suddenly become tight at the hips and around the chest, his boots become too big and his hat too small. From his corner in the northwest, he saw how his eyes became speckled like two snake eggs. The dying Lieutenant Sofronije Opujić was turning into his own mother, Madam Paraskeva.

And then, underneath her son's shirt, which was tight on her, Madam Paraskeva suddenly felt Sofronije's small hunger under the heart as her own pain and afterwards that pain under the heart as Sofronije's hunger. So it was that Sofronije remembered his wish and recovered.

Yes, half of life comes to us, the other half goes to meet its maker. And so it should be, thought the young Opujić. He smiled and fingered his moustache, which had been freshly plaited like a whip. Someone had combed it while he was ill.

Then he was taken to Zemun.

$\mathcal{D}$EATH

$\mathcal{A}$s soon as he crossed the Elbe in the mud and the rain under enemy fire, Captain Haralampije Opujić set up camp in a small deserted castle near the town of Torgau. The light of eight Gothic windows cut into eight parts the oval room that served as the library, and it also cut into eight parts every cannon-shot heard from the battlefront. The other parts of the chamber were shrouded in semi-darkness and silence. Galleries circled the bookshelves, and planted right in the middle of the stone floor was an immense tub shaped like a copper flower. Lolling like a bear in the hot salted water was Captain Haralampije Opujić, washing off the mud and the blood and purring like a cat, slurping his honeyed cold nettle tea. An orderly quickly placed a board across the tub and a small wooden mallet on the board. With practised fingers he braided plaits in the captain's beard, slid the board under them and gave them a good hammering with the mallet, to dry them out and pound them into a nice shape. Then he put a white towel over the board and served Captain Opujić a light dinner – first a bit of cheese, made of women's and goat's milk and soaked in oil, with a salad of male (penile) tomatoes and onions, followed by prosciutto and a glass of Tokai wine from the cellars of Haralampije's friends, the Vitkovićes. The captain had carried the wine with him through the war from Eger to Russia and back across the Elbe . . .

In the middle of dinner Captain Opujić suddenly burst out with the words: '*De figuris sententiarum!* How does it go?'

And he began to count, folding the fingers of his left hand: '*Interogatio, subjectio, anteoccupatio, correctio, dubitatio* . . . How does it continue? . . . It's a good thing we still have hair growing on our heads and not grass,' remarked the captain to his orderly, 'and on that note, *mon cher*, have a glass of Tokai, and let us read *The Iliad*.'

'Yes, sir,' replied the orderly, reading out the title: '*The Iliad*.'

Behind the seas, near Troy, lies a water which is bitter and unpotable. Thirsty animals gather at this watering place, but they cannot drink until the unicorn arrives. His horn is medicinal and when he lowers his head to drink, the horn stirs the water, making it murky but sweet to drink. And then the other thirsty animals drink alongside him. And when he quenches his thirst and lifts his horn out of the water, the water becomes as bitter as it was before. But while the uni-

corn is stirring the water with his horn, he clears it further with his eyes and visible in that clearness, as if laid out in the palm of one's hand, is the future of the world. My brother Jelen Priamužević had himself come many a time to this water and waited with the animals for the unicorn to appear . . .

'Is that true, have you really got a brother?' interrupted Captain Opujić from his bath.

'He's not my brother, *mon seigneur*. He's the brother of the man in the book,' said the orderly.

'Read on then.'

My brother Jelen Priamužević had himself come many a time to this water and waited with the animals for the unicorn to appear. And once, while the others were drinking their fill, he saw the spot in the water which had cleared the unicorn's eyes. And suddenly an endless array of senseless absurdities spread open before his idle, cowardly eyes, and he saw them so clearly that they filled up his very being. He saw further and further through the days which welled forth like waves and kept telling us what he saw. And what he saw was his Saturday beard grow prematurely on Sunday, so that he could not grab and scratch it. Land opened up before him, future vegetation rustled in his ears and the taste of the rocks began to simmer in his mouth. Counting the sunny years, he saw how Adam and Eve's fiery apple moved to our city of Troy. And he saw me, his brother Paris Pastirević Alexander, older than I am, sticking a shepherd's staff in my hat, changing my socks and going to Sparta where, with my finger dipped in wine, I write on the table an offer of love to another man's beautiful wife, Helen is her name. And then he saw how I would steal that woman like a

*sheep and bring her to our city of Troy and how Troy would
accept the fiery apple and burn down to the ground . . .*

'How did you get the name Paris Pastirević? He was a
handsome man, that's why Helen followed him, but
you, look at yourself, were it not for your ears you
would be smiling through your hair.'

'That is not my name, *mon seigneur*. That is the
name of the man in the book.'

'You just said it was yours. Continue reading and
don't make any more mistakes with names!'

*Penetrating still further, ever deeper through time, my
brother Jelen vić saw all sorts of absurd nonsense, and he
could not stop plunging through his eyes and that clear
water into a time when those eyes and that water would be
no more, like a sock pulled inside out. He had learned from
the palm tree that standing was more painful than anything
else, but he continued to stand at the window of his death
between his ears and he saw the Crusaders in
Constantinople in 1204 loading four fat bronze horses on
to Venetian galleys, he saw the frightened Paleologues and
Slavs all shod in mud plunging their spears into the wood-
en gates of Constantinople, and he saw the decline of an
empire. He saw Rome move to Constantinople and he saw
Rome in Moscow and the ship of Cosma who sailed to India,
and Columbus's ship on the shores of the New World, he saw
the Turks at the doors of Vienna and the French in Venice
where they removed the four horses of Constantinople from
St Mark's Church, and he saw the decline of yet another
empire . . .*

'You're lying! *L'Empire de Napoleon* is not declining!'

'Did our side remove those horses or not?'
'Go on reading so we can discover what happens.'

And he saw the Gauls in Byelorussia full of horse
meat and the battle at Leipzig and Napoleon on two
islands . . .

'Nonsense! How can our emperor be on any islands?
And what battle is that at Leipzig? Why, that is near
here! It's within spitting distance. I don't understand
a thing about the future . . . That was never my strong
suit. My job is not the future. My job is death. Verily.'

*And from the ramparts of Troy my crazy brother Jelen
Priamužević saw Schliemann and the red snows of an
October in Russia, he saw the persecution of the Jews and
the blitzkrieg and the four men at Yalta and Stalin in 1948
and, terrified, tearing away the mists of his sins, he saw
Jerusalem and the Wailing Wall and the Arabs, and oil
flowing again from the East, and Anglo-Saxons on the
Moon, in space where the Soviet Russians are, and Serbs
before the entire world, and who knows what else and how
far he saw, draining the well of his prophetic eyes . . . At that
moment, I suddenly became tired of all these ruses and ram-
blings and I actually did stick my shepherd's staff into my
hat and, changing my socks, went to Sparta to dip my finger in wine and write on the table my offer of love to that
beautiful woman, Helen Basileus. Let what has been seen
begin!*

Just then the captain noticed that the water had gone
cold.
'Clarinetto!' he boomed, standing up to his full

height so suddenly that half the water splashed out of the tub. He pulled tight his naked body with a Comorin belt, spun out of red woollen cord, and got into bed. Then he was given his clarinet and an already burning green pipe. He took a puff or two, sitting in bed with the instrument lying across his knees. A soldier appeared holding the same instrument in his hand.

'Is it true,' the captain asked the soldier, 'that you have nimble fingers, that you can steal the shoe off a running man?'

'That's a lie. What would I do with one shoe? But I can teach you, captain, both the one and the other. Both to play and to steal. Whichever you prefer.'

Captain Haralampije Opujić burst into such laughter that it sent the ashes flying and his pipe burned out. He grabbed the clarinet and in unison with the soldier played Paisiello.

Captain Haralampije Opujić of the French cavalry learned, in the middle of his campaign, how to play the clarinet. And he learned Latin rhetoric as well. His progress, unlike the French army's, was not bad. Perhaps that was why Captain Opujić's transformation did not raise an eyebrow. There was too much death around the Elbe for such things to be noticed.

⟋EMPERANCE

ᴸIEUTENANT Opujić recovered some time just before spring. Reality and dreams were still completely oblivious of each other, but he knew his name again. He caught his thoughts like flies, with little success. They usually escaped him. And when he did catch them, they either lay dead in his hand or else, crippled, would try to fly away. He noticed that instead of proud flesh on his wound a tuft of red hair, like a pigtail, was now growing on his chest.

By his side he found a servant sent, he was told, by his father and his old pouch, albeit empty. The only valuable Sofronije carried in it had disappeared. The bracelet his mother had given him for his 'future intended' was gone. The servant knew nothing about it, but he did mention a girl who had tended to the lieutenant during his illness.

'She's probably one of those your father sends to heal and lick you like a bitch, if you'll pardon the expression.'

Opujić asked where he could find the woman, but the servant said that he did not know her, that she had stopped coming after he arrived. With a dismissive wave of his hand the lieutenant left, having first asked the servant the name of the city they were in.

'Zemun,' replied the surprised servant.

In the street outside, Opujić put on his gloves for the first time in half a year and felt something hard inside. It was a ring, a completely unfamiliar ring. A man's signet ring, the young Opujić noticed. He put it on his finger, over the glove, and began scanning the street for a red-headed woman. Luck was not with him that day, but the next morning not far from his residence he caught sight of a girl whose red braid glittered in the sun as if plaited with copper wire. Instead of ornaments, she wore expensive gold and silver thimbles on her fingers, and in place of a necklace a tiny silver-woven shoe around her neck.

'Impossible!' Sofronije exclaimed to himself and followed her.

She went down to the Danube, removed one of her shoes and dipped her foot in the water to see whether it was cold, and for a moment she was both on land and in the river; then she turned around, ran up the steps and disappeared through a door studded with four horseshoes. He registered that the horseshoes stood opposite each other, like two horses face to face.

111

The next day, however, he saw the girl again. She was within arm's reach, sitting on the balcony of that same building, her back turned to him and to the passers-by, deftly braiding and unbraiding the red hair that cascaded down her back. The lieutenant was shocked when he recognized his bracelet on her arm. Only then did he take a better look at the girl. He liked her narrow feet and long toes and thought, This one has a hard cunt . . . And he passed by the balcony, but later he returned; he could not get her out of his mind. She was still there and in her boredom was pouring wine back and forth between a silver and a gold goblet. Aware of one goblet but not of the other, she sat there pensively, her leg sticking through the balcony railing.

You can tell from her hands that she will have two children, thought Opujić, from the way she wears her dress that she will divorce and from the way she combs her hair I would say that she will die at the age of forty-eight. Just as musicians think with their ears, so this one thinks with her tits, the young Opujić decided as he addressed the girl.

'You stole my bracelet! It's right there on your arm!'

She turned her gaze on him and he noticed that her body began to smell of peaches. That look made her plaits start to rise like two snakes.

'Anyone can say that. Prove it.'

'I'll tell you what is inscribed on the bracelet. It says: '*I am an amulet. If you empty me I shall no longer be of use to you. If you learn how to refill me, I shall be of use to you again. But beware, the fact that the amulet does not serve you is not to say that it does not serve others . .* '

'That is what is inscribed on my bracelet. And it's

your hard luck! You will have to give it back to me, even though that bracelet devours the arm that wears it! When you remove it, you will be left without an arm.'

The girl on the balcony merely giggled.

'Then I won't remove it. We'll swap.'

'Swap what?'

'Just as you claim that I stole your bracelet from you, so I claim that you stole my ring. It's right there on your finger. The signet ring that is used to fill a pipe. It has its own round gold inscription.

The lieutenant looked at the ring and read the inscription to himself: *'Remember me! The ring is virginity renewed. If you lose me . . .'*, whereupon he heard the girl on the balcony say aloud, *'Remember me! The ring is virginity renewed. If you lose me you shall lose more than me. I await your finger as your groom.'*

Suddenly he seemed to wake up. He heard the small hunger under his heart weep like a small pain and, deep beneath the cobblestones with their green overgrowth, he heard the dead browsing on the grass from underneath, from the roots. His hair bristled and he asked: 'Who are you?'

'I am the third shoe,' said the girl, disappearing into the house with the horseshoes on its front door.

The young Opujić agonized over that ring for two nights, and on the third he took a piece of chalk and drew a male cross on the door with the four horseshoes. In the morning the girl sent a servant to ask what the sign meant.

'Is it a threat?'

'No, it is not a threat, on the contrary, it means that there is no life for me on this side of that door.'

The next morning the girl took a piece of chalk and drew a female cross on the inside of the door, and towards evening she opened the door outwards so that Sofronije could see the sign, and see it he did. He heard the girl somewhere inside singing softly, as if through the moonlight, the song 'Memories Are the Sweat of the Soul'. And he walked in. She offered him candied flowers – some roses and violets.

'Who are you?' he asked her again.

'Who am I? My name is Jerisena Tenecki. But I am less and less sure of who I am and more and more surprised by what I do and what I am becoming. Instead of knowing myself better and better, I know myself less and less. I am becoming a stranger in my own life. And I'm glad of it . . . And who are you?'

'There are moments on the river just before nightfall, when both bird and fish attack the same fly. I am such a fly, and this is such a moment by the river. But don't think that I don't care who devours me. You or somebody else.'

As he uttered these words, Sofronije noticed that her whole body was beginning to smell of peaches again and he kissed her.

'What's that you've got under your tongue,' she asked startled. 'A stone?'

'Yes, that's where I keep my secret.'

'Give it to me, give me your secret!' she said, and in their next kiss the pebble changed mouths and moved to hers. Speaking over the pebble Jerisena then said: 'Every evening an angel pulls my soul out of my life and body like a huge net with all its catch. Last night it netted something new. Using my soul it caught yours.'

He discovered that she painted her lips and the nipples on her breasts the same colour, and at exactly midnight he discharged twelve spurts of his seed into her, in unison with the strokes of the tower clock.

Thus began a great love. And one ages rapidly from great loves. One ages more rapidly from a great love than from a long, hard and unhappy life. Jerisena rode on her horseman across faraway unknown lands, returning tired, happy and breathless from the long journey. Thereafter her womb responded to the strokes of the bell. Love left her no time to eat. Sometimes she would lay out evening breakfast on her lover's chest and, seated on top of him, would eat, feeding him simultaneously with love and mashed beans. They were happy in the midst of general misery, successful in the midst of general defeat, and they would never be forgiven for it.

The Third Seven Keys

The Devil

DEUCE was born on a bridge over the Karaš river in Banat, when his master in boredom rechristened his own shadow. He was given countless names, such as Unmentionable, Him There, Rock in His Teeth, God's Brother, the Evil One. But he felt that he was the same as the name and was afraid of someone throwing the note on which his name was written into the fire. He liked to pee with his tail, he never planted pumpkins alone, and others liked to spit in his ear.

He grew up by Lake Bukumir in Montenegro, among the rocks. He could write, but he could not read, because if he read his name it would immediately kill him. All that would remain of him would be a hollow bone. He did not like roses and he did not like his black teeth to show, so he never smiled. He wore strange boots, their heels were turned back to front, he was said to resemble himself and to be swifter than an angel, although he had a slight limp. He was seen tracing circles around children with that tail of his. When he was little he would hide in men's trouser cuffs and under women's skirts, frightened by lightning, because he believed that the bolts of lightning were looking just for him. He liked to observe his reflection in axe blades, and when it thundered people would bring out their axes with his reflection in them and thus stop the lightning from striking their homes.

His particular area of authority, they say, was when it was someone's turn to be vampired a third time. He would then lead that someone, that thrice-born vampire, through people's dreams teaching them to stutter. He liked to ride adults and milk other people's cattle, he dressed as a woman, wrapped his tail around his waist and introduced himself as the fiancée of some boy from town. He had his own barber and lots of brothers scattered all over the world. Each of his brothers spoke a different language.

He planted blackberries, could have the last laugh, cook someone's goose and cut trips short. Children wet their beds when they dreamed about him. He knew the language of animals, loved music, was hated by women who sealed him up in a bottle because they thought he carried a man's head on a woman's body, but they would sell him even their souls because he knew that Eve had been expelled from Eden long after Adam, and, furthermore, he could lash out with his tail or whatever it was that he whisked out of his trousers. He was a good ploughman; he could plough up the bottom of a river. He feared black dogs, the cock's crow, and he liked to sit on the scale in the water-mill. He never sought company; it sought him, even though people were afraid of him. They would say, 'If he grabs your skirt – cut it off!'

He was afraid of hawthorns and knives in black sheaths. He cast the shadow of a horse and was at home everywhere, but the children made fun of him, shouting 'Twee, twee! Go graze on white mares!'

In his youth, he once made a wolf out of a rod and a goatskin, but the wolf never got off the ground. Then in his dream he prayed to God, because he believed in God only in his dreams. And God said to him, 'Tell your wolf: "Jump on the father!" and he will come to life.'

That is what he did and the wolf almost tore him to pieces.

Fishermen gave him Communion by not swallowing it in the church, but rather spitting it into the river and saying 'I give you Communion, you give me fish!'

People said he was a slanderer, but he was afraid of dog-roses, spotted puppies and black belts. If somebody slapped him, he would turn the other cheek to be slapped as well, but since people knew that this was not done they never dared hit him twice, because then two more of his kind would be born. That they left to the women, who beat him hard enough to make his tail drop off and when that finally happened, he made such a beautiful girl out of his tail that no one was her equal. Her name was Petra Alaup and she lived in Trieste. At crossroads he would boast, 'God made man in his image and likeness and look how ugly man is; I made my sister out of my tail and look what a beauty she is.'

One stormy night he took her as his wife and for three months she kept the cock's egg in her armpit and did not wash. The egg hatched a child with cow ears. It was the spitting image of its father. In addition to that child, Deuce also had another. He was the father of the lie. He never wrought evil against somebody who hated him, only against his own family and those who loved him. His biography was compiled in *Niš* (Pavle Sofrić, 'History of the Serb Devil', *Niš Eparchy Herald*).

In 1813 he got tired of the blacksmith's trade and asked his wife Petra Alaup what he should do. She whispered from her mouth into his. He then put on yellow Turkish peasant shoes, rode off on his white mare and enlisted in Napoleon's cavalry. He was assigned to Captain Haralampije Opujić's unit, which was in the process of losing the war at Leipzig.

$\mathcal{T}$HE $\mathcal{T}$OWER

$\mathcal{O}$NE morning the rooms in the buildings of Zemun dawned all bright from the snow that had fallen overnight and the white glare in the wall mirror made Sofronije and Jerisena wake up early.

At breakfast that snowy morning he asked her, 'Why doesn't your older brother ever visit us?'

'Because he is the Austrian officer who stabbed you with the scabbard of his sword and had you hung from a tree. He is far away. Chasing the French.'

'And you tell me that only now? Why did you rescue me?'

Watching him chew one mouthful like his maternal grandfather and the other like his paternal grandmother, she said, 'There are two types of women. In that respect it's as if women have two different sexes, like two shoes on their feet.

'You can call the first type the Victor's Wife. She has no father. And she always accedes to her husband, whom she adores as someone powerful, as Adam and the father of her offspring, as triumphing over the world of animals, to which he gave names, and over nature, which he fought. She has not forgotten where the earth's navel lies. She has power and money through her husband. His days are long and have more nights in them than I have, she muses thinking about her man, and she despises her sons for being soft and disunited, like Cain and Abel, loners with no power or influence. Let them plough up their shadows and water them with sweat to make them grow, she muses, thinking about her offspring. And she hates their peers as well, that entire generation which plugs its ears with its beard. When she chooses, she chooses not the one she most loves, but the one her father or son most hate. Her love is tied to the clitoris and means pleasure regardless of conception.

'You can call the other type of woman the Victor's Daughter. She is in love with the Father, who can say of himself: "Before ever I was, I was learned." In him she sees a creator, victor, power-wielder who deftly weaves the kinship of unanimity around himself and her. She despises her own husband. Although he may be a good man and a great expert in his field, of him this woman says: "Everyone can rap him on his watch and wring his soul dry with music, a thistle will grow out of his ear!" She does not forgive him for being a loner. Who needs somebody with no power or influence, somebody with less authority than a eunuch! For these same reasons, she despises her brothers and their peers. They were under the cap of time and then removed the cap, she says of them. But she adores her son and his peers, because their days have twins, in them she sees a new great kinship connected by the same spirit as her father's brotherhood, in them she sees future victors. They have removed all four dried sweats and all four winds beneath them and now they are free, she thinks, because in her case power and wealth are gained through either the father or the son. She usually winds up in the bed of one of her son's friends. When she chooses she chooses not the one she most loves but the one her husband or brother most hate . . . Her love is tied to the uterus and means conception regardless of pleasure.

'And you, to which of these two types do you belong? Which sex are you?' he asked her in trepidation.

'Neither. In a certain sense I am sexless. And, for the time being at least, I am the exception. I am the third shoe. When I choose, I choose the one I most love.'

'So the third shoe really does exist!'

'Yes. I try not to behave like other women. I do not obey the laws of generational change between the victors and the vanquished, because that is the behavioural norm of the male species. I know that for men the world happens in someone else and for women it happens within themselves. I know that when the shadows of the evening plants soar to the sky, I am the Daughter of the Vanquished. And in spite of everybody, I adore my father.'

'But don't you know that my father killed your

father some time in the last war and the last century?'

'You cannot be blamed for that, but my brother can – Captain Pana Tenecki of the Austrian army, who is as bloodthirsty as your father, Captain Haralampije Opujić of the French cavalry. In their case, the blame can be carried back through time. That is why I cannot stand that arrogant phalanx of my brothers and their tyrant, victor friends, and they, in turn, cannot stand me. Nor can their wives. I shudder to even think of my children and theirs, who will be subjected to their triumphant violence if they win this war which you and yours are losing. I would like, if I can, to wind up in the bed of one of my future son's weak peers, more as a mother than as a mistress, just as I chose you as the weak son of a strong, victorious father. I chose you because you were not loved by your mother or sisters or mistresses, and you will not be loved by your daughter if ever we have one. It will be my greatest defeat and worst punishment if I fail, if I am forced to return to the powerful flock of my victorious brothers, to which all my female peers belong and to which your father belonged as well. It will be the end of the road for me if I have to remove the third shoe.

'But never mind about me. Let us see where you and the two of us stand. You want to return to your unit which remains on the retreat, marching north-westwards. That is bound to finish somewhere in France. I do not know whether France is your state or not, but I do know that you serve in its army. I also know that states are a necessary evil. The most you can expect of a state is for it not to spit in your soup. And wars? The nation, you say, you are fighting for the glory of your nation. What is the nation? Look at me. I am seventeen years old. I am the contemporary of mankind, because mankind is always seventeen years old. That means that a nation is a perpetual child. It keeps growing and its language, its spirit, its memory, its future even, are always too small for it, like clothes. Which is why a nation must keep changing its attire, because it always becomes too short, too tight, and bursts at the seams. And that is something both difficult and joyful. Language you say. In our dreams we all understand every language. Dreams are our pre-Tower of Babylon homeland. In our dreams we all speak the one and only great primeval language of us all, both living and dead . . . So what is the point of war? Why travel through history backwards? Every murder is part of a suicide.'

'Are you trying to persuade me to leave my military calling?'

'Yes. I want you to leave the military. It is your father's calling, not yours. Let us leap from that tower into the flames, from that defeat and disaster which you vainly believe protect us and gives us security and money. Let us start from the beginning.'

'You know what, my dear, I learned something in war. Those of my peers in the unit who were to die earlier were wiser and knew more about the world around them than the others, and that is how we recognized them and sensed that they would soon be killed. They knew that every murder is committed with a thousand years of premeditation . . . The others, who were to die later, were more stupid. But none of that had anything to do with the innate brightness or dull-wittedness of the ones or the others. So, there are two cases. We belong to the latter.'

'How do you mean?'

'We are happy lovers. Aren't we? And happiness makes one stupid. Happiness and wisdom do not go together, just as body and thought do not go together. Because only pain is the thought of the body. In other words, happy people become stupid people. It is only when they get tired of their happiness that lovers can become wise again, if that is what they otherwise are. So let us not decide now about unbelting my sabre . . . Your steps are the master, and you are their servant . . .'

Thus spoke the foolish young Lieutenant Opujić of Trieste on that winter morning in Zemun, never noticing that his sabre was already unbelted.

$\mathcal{T}$HE $\mathcal{S}$TAR

$\mathcal{W}$HEN Lieutenant Sofronije Opujić unbelted his sabre and renounced his military ways, he and Jerisena Tenecki settled down on a piece of land and cultivated it. This particular evening they ate some wonderful, slightly spicy young honey from their bee-hive, pressed moon and a pie made of wild chestnuts and bitter oranges. They were lying in bed, talking in the dark about stars stupid and wise. The window was open, the curtain was plunging deep into the room, swelling as if pregnant, and inside it was the still wind. Sofronije remembered how when he was a child in Trieste he would swing on the huge gate, holding on to the handle with his chin and hands; but then, as always, they immersed themselves in a thousand and one nights. They tried to calculate which was the night that Scheherazade had conceived her child with Harun and which story she had recounted that evening. But their calculation never turned out properly, because they always had too few nights and never enough sleep. They lived rapidly – four seasons every day, as Jerisena was wont to say.

That night they also had another topic on which to exchange thoughts. Captain Haralampije Opujić had written, confiding that he was reading Horatio, playing the clarinet and, among a thousand other such juicy titbits, said that he would like to see them: his future daughter-in-law for the first time and his son once more after so many years, so that he would know him if he ever ran into him. The father had been transferred to a unit which was escorting an emissary on a diplomatic mission to Constantinople and the trip would be taking them through the region where Jerisena and Sofronije lived . . . But, to Jerisena's great surprise, the young Opujić hesitated in answering his father's letter. Sometimes she thought Sofronije was hiding something from her.

He was indeed hiding something. The same thing he was hiding from everybody else, from the whole world – the small hunger under his heart which turned at the bottom of his soul into a small pain. Occasionally he would shut himself up alone in his room and do something, wait for the post or go off somewhere for a day or two. And at night he would listen and hear the music of the magnetic storms whose gusts and echoes revealed to him subterranean passages, labyrinths and entire towns long since destroyed and wiped off the face of the earth, and he would roam their buried streets, guided by the laughter of the cold and hot smells of the underground. Or he would hear through the rock and sand the unison humming of the blood groups of ore that was simply the echo of continents long since submerged under the Panonian Sea. A sea that no longer existed but which protected its connection with both Atlantises like umbilical cords . . .

Jerisena, reflected here in the eyes of cows and goats, in the eyes of snakes and dogs, noticed that there was a restlessness inside him. His behaviour and conversations were always different in each room of their house, where the locks and handles cracked like empty pistols. Behind every door he became someone else. In the kitchen he spoke only Turkish; in the drawing-room he spoke the language of Jerisena's mother, which he had learned from his mistress; in the study he kept silent. At night he would lie down in bed naked and as hot as burning ember, but once asleep he would slowly cool down like a huge stove and before dawn, when he ranted in Greek, she would have to cover him like a child.

One afternoon she kissed him and he flinched.

'What's that you have in your mouth?' he asked.

'A pebble with your secret inside it. Have you forgotten that your secret is with me? I've been taking good care of it all this time. So now tell me what it is. It has been shut away inside you for too long, like a message in a bottle. Why do you worry about your secret anyway? Every secret is kept by its own timidity. Let it look after itself.'

'All right,' he decided, 'by the morning of the day after tomorrow, when you bring the freshly baked bread to the workers and me out on the estate, I will think of a way. Because it is not a trifling matter . . .'

And so it was done. He went out to the estate, bringing the labourers brandy infused with seven different herbs. On the second morning the workers got hungry early and before Jerisena had arrived with the bread. When they asked Sofronije for something to appease their hunger, he was delighted. They were sitting under a fig tree, and so he said, 'Bear fruit, fig, so for workers to have something to eat!'

The words were from a story he had heard as a child.

And the tree actually did bear several figs two months prematurely and so they ate. Jerisena, bearing the bread loaves and offerings on the cart for that morning, arrived two months later . . .

Carrying on her shoulders two pitchers she had taken from the cart, she walked with one foot in the water and the other on the shore of the lake bordering the property. She never even noticed that so much time had elapsed. She was more beautiful than ever.

'Have you thought of a way?' she asked him, whispering to herself, 'Such bitterness in the mouth, as if the whole soul resided in there!'

'Yes, I have thought of a way,' he replied. 'You will listen with your mouth, not with your ears.'

'What do you mean?'

'That's the way. I will recite a poem to you in my language, and you will listen to it in your mother tongue.'

'They are not the same language,' she replied.

'That's the whole point. If you are ready to listen, you will discover the truth in the silence between the two languages. Oceans of silence reign between languages. I have arranged it so that the words you hear will sound the same in my language as they do in your mother's language, but in her language they will mean something completely different. And they will reveal my secret. Their meaning in my language is utterly irrelevant.'

And so he began:

'I pray to thee, Mother of God, Queen of Heaven,
Turn not thine eyes upon her, upon my love,
And heed not her pleas
And mention her not in thy prayers!
Let thy soul imperceptibly fly
Over what she shall do.
For what my love shall do
Is so terrible I dare not
Even contemplate or learn what it is.
And if thou shouldst intercede for her, for my love,
Thou shalt know everything about her, that I dare not know.
If thou prayest for her and her sins,
Then I too must know of them, I who now pray to thee.
I pray to thee, Mother of God, Queen of Heavens,
Turn not thine eyes upon her, upon my love!

Jerisena listened to him carefully and her brow slowly cleared, for she realized that his great desire did not contain a woman, or rather that it contained all women along with everyone else inside them. She realized it was something else that was drawing him into the future, something truly enchanting and irresistible. As soon as they arrived home, she took Sofronije's yellow cavalry boots out of the wardrobe and packed their travel bags.

'We're going with your father to Constantinople. Straight to that pillar with the copper shield.'

KEY 18

The Moon

IT was the time of year known as 'between two breads' when Jerisena Tenecki and her lover set off for the East, toward the quarantine, where they were to wait at an inn for Captain Haralampije Opujić and the delegation he was escorting. Jerisena slept in the carriage, which was laden with supplies, and the young Opujić rode on horseback. The entire time he could feel two roads ringing out from under his horse's hooves; the road of the Roman legions, charging eastward, rang out like an audible shadow beneath the upper road leading to Constantinople.

The journey took them through a region known in winter as 'between dog and wolf', and in the distance they saw two towers, one on each side of the road,

134

when suddenly they heard gunshots. Opujić spurred his horse and behind the bend in the road saw a river. It smelt of roe and was afloat with walnuts which were so plentiful that year that they broke the boughs they hung from, their fruits and leaves filling the water below. Lying on the river like a spider suspended from the smoke of its red chimney stack was a huge decaying inn, and in front of it some travellers were shooting at something in the water.

'Don't, d-don't let it, d-don't let it get across!' cried one of them, stammering.

'Oh God, there it is, it made it!' groaned another, recharging his rifle.

Sofronije Opujić decided that this must simply be some sort of idle fun and he entered the inn to inquire about a room.

'There is just one room,' said the innkeeper, leading Jerisena and Sofronije to the floor upstairs, which was ringed by a cobble-stoned balcony. The cobblestones were already overgrown with grass, and the room had once been painted green. It had a stove which was heated from the outside with a brick of dung and straw, and inside the water was heated on a bench.

'The best room in the inn,' said the boy, but he was looking sideways somehow, as if he was about to spit.

'I see you do target practice here,' said Sofronije over dinner to the man who had done most of the shouting down by the river.

'You d-don't understand, sir,' replied the man. 'Tomorrow when you find your feet, you'll b-b-begin shooting too. Tell me, which r-room have they given you?'

'Not the green room?' interrupted the other traveller. 'You know, if you are in the green room, be careful what you dream tonight.'

'And why should I, may I ask?' replied Opujić, laughing.

'All of us waiting here in quarantine have already passed through that room. And immediately asked for another. Whoever spent the night in that room dreamed the same thing.'

'And what is that, I would like to know?' Sofronije continued in the same joking tone.

'What a stubborn creature you are!' said the third man. 'They dreamed, my dear fellow, about one and the same man who smells of walnuts. His pigtail is held by a nacre butterfly. The man wears an officer's tunic and tries to kill anyone who dreams about him in that room. He tried to get me with his sabre too, but I woke up in time. Some people didn't.'

'And what happened to them?'

'They s-stammer,' replied the man from the riverbank. 'That's w-why we shoot.'

'What do you shoot at?' asked Jerisena, laughing as well.

'At walnut shells. They're used by evil spirits to carry them across the water from Turkey. Because evil spirits cannot cross water themselves. So they get walnut shells to carry them . . . Yesterday one of the guests, who is from Zemun, dreamed about and recognized the one from the green room. He said the fellow he dreamed about owns a bell foundry in Zemun.'

'Bah, witches use a walnut shell for a boat and you want to stop the witchman! It's no use! Their kind will cross the water in an eggshell,' said Jerisena, laughing at them all, but the next morning she too woke up pale.

That night she and the young Opujić went to bed early. Lying on her back in the green moonlight she could feel the smells piling up on the river, the lighter ones on top of the heavy ones: first the smell of tar, water and mud, then smoke and lastly, floating on the river's surface, chunky smells of lime tree. Even the moonlight had three smells, it was a blend of all three phases of the moon that night. The damp of the water came in through the windows and somewhere in the inn someone had started playing the clarinet. Very softly he was playing their song 'Memories Are the Sweat of the Soul,' and Sofronije Opujić took a lock of Jerisena's hair in his mouth. Lying on his stomach, amazed by this music in such a place, he felt that he and this terrible desire inside him were ageing, that the nights took him back to some time in the past, the days pulled him in the opposite direction and the future was like a darkness slowly receding before his every step. He worried about Jerisena for no tangible reason, he felt the taste of dust under his bed and decay under the inn. He heard the crabs come out on to the shore in the moonlight and his sense of smell plunged deeper and deeper, encountering the underground smells of damp silver and burnt rock. He could feel how the subterranean gases drove the petroleum up the inclines of the earth's womb, how the smells of decaying plants, sulphur and hot iron-rich water piled on top of each other. Just before daybreak, Jerisena, lying in bed next to him, screamed and woke him up:

'What a place! Senseless rain, senseless sun! I

dreamed about him,' she said.

'How do you know it was him?'

'He had that nacre butterfly in his pigtail . . . He had a book tucked under his belt, they were verses I think . . .'

'Did he attack you?'

'No. On the contrary, the sight of me scared him to death.'

Suddenly a fresh gunshot was fired outside. Opujić got up, looked over the balcony railing and froze. The travellers from the inn were shooting straight at Sofronije's father. Jerisena cried out, 'That's him! I recognized him! There's the nacre butterfly in his hair!'

To which Sofronije retorted: 'Quiet! That's my father and those blockheads want to kill him!'

He grabbed a rifle.

But Captain Haralampije Opujić was in no need of help. His cavalrymen disarmed the group in a flash, gave the stammerer who had fired at the captain a good, hard slap, which stopped his stammer, and led the French envoy's sumptuous carriage into the court-yard of the inn. It was covered with an inch of gilding and two inches of mud. When they opened the carriage door and lowered the steps, the first thing to appear was a purple boot, whereupon a boy jumped down dressed in a blue tunic belted with a silk veil, and the whisper went around that he was the envoy of his imperial majesty Napoleon and was going to Constantinople on assignment.

THE SUN

'THE two of you are beautiful and happy. I wish you everything that has already happened to you,' said Captain Haralampije Opujić when his son presented Jerisena.

Opujić the elder was sitting in the inn wearing the bloodstained spurs which that morning had saved his life from the unexpected bullet and smoking his green pipe. He was as sturdy as a tile stove, even though he was ageing in 'bursts of time', at first nothing for ten years and then ten years in one night. He could carry a donkey across a bridge, as he liked to joke; the travellers in quarantine stared fearfully at his pigtail and the nacre butterfly that adorned it and sniffed at the smell of walnuts he always emanated; Jerisena gazed in amazement at the little collection of Horatio's verse tucked under the captain's belt. He, meanwhile, cheerfully ordered dinner for everyone in the inn, including the envoy who was supping in his own room.

The French envoy had taken his secretary with him on the trip to Constantinople, but the captain had with him five horsemen in red boots, as if going to a wedding, and a sixth one in yellow Turkish peasant shoes. They were capable of overtaking, escaping and being with the worst. Captain Opujić had also brought along a girl with strange flowers of grey in her raven-black hair, a girl so buxom that she could bite off her own tit. They called her Dunja. As soon as she saw Jerisena and the young Opujić, Dunja giggled at the third shoe hanging around Jerisena's neck and asked Sofronije how his wound was doing. Jerisena thus realized that the girl from the captain's entourage was one of the healers the father had sent across three battlefields to the son, and she recognized in Dunja's hair the lock that was growing on her own Sofronije's shoulder; sprinkled with the same little stars of grey.

'Do you remember how we dined with Jevdokija?' Dunja asked Sofronije, resting her two golden eyes, which looked like two halves of a boiled egg, upon Jerisena.

'Let's see,' said the captain, enjoying his dinner in advance, folding the fingers on his hand which was heavy even without any rings (because rings interfere with the sabre).

'Let's see. First, a portion of grey grass and tongue in bran soup for everyone . . . And, if you've got it, bring us some bread made with a dash of earth. Regarding love for one's fatherland, my son, it's like

140

this: everything for the people, nothing with the people! And you, boy, whip me up two bowls of warm God's tears, a breaded gaze, the bitter kind that ages in an hour, with lemon. And beans boiled in Sava river water. You don't have Sava water? That's a pity! Then give me breaded horsebeans . . . And for Miss Tenecki some breaded mussels. For my Dunja whatever Jevdokija wants. And, to top it all off, some nettle tea with honey.'

'Can that be my father? Sofronije wondered, remembering his childhood and how in the bed chamber of their palace in Trieste his father would lie in the dark beside his wife Paraskeva Opujić and raise his head to listen. Sofronije now finally knew what his father had been listening to all those years ago. And he knew why his mother would lower his father's head back on to the pillow in the darkness of night. Opujić the elder had been listening for the rustling of a skirt at the bottom of the staircase.

'As for those in Servia,' the captain went on, 'I send them the money I earn wasting French gunpowder so that they can buy gunpowder of their own. You, boy, sharpen these knives until I can slice the wick off a burning candle with them. And pick out some black spoons for us. I prefer black spoons, they are the most beautiful, are they not, Miss Tenecki? Come on, hurry up, hurry up, boy! At daybreak everybody here has a journey to pack on his back and it's he who takes to his heels first . . .'

The captain had not even finished ordering when a bunch of women burst into the inn with a bear and a man in a French tunic in tow. They introduced themselves as a travelling theatre.

'This performance, you should know, has been paid for by our benefactor, Captain Haralampije Opujić,' said the man in the tunic. 'He is a great admirer of the stage and is somewhere in Silesia right now. We shall therefore perform for you a terrible play called *The Three Deaths of Captain Opujić*.'

Captain Opujić greeted these words with a gale of laughter and turned to address the actors:

'Perform, my children, and may your paper words find repose in our dreams, may they find warmth in our blood and for a second be afflicted with life again!'

Then one of the women turned to the false Captain Opujić, the one in the French tunic, and said:

'Your ancestors, captain, had only one death each. But not you! You will have three deaths and here they are' (whereupon she indicated the other three women in the troupe). 'This old lady here, this beauty and this little girl here, they are your three deaths. Take a good look at them . . .'

'And that is all that will be left of me?' the real Captain Opujić said, interrupting the play.

'Yes. That is all.'

'It is quite a lot!' interjected Captain Opujić again.

'But, beware, captain, you will not notice your deaths, you will ride through them like through the gate of triumph and you will continue your journey as if nothing had happened.'

'What happens after my third death, after I am vampired a third time?' the captain broke in, again revelling in the consternation of the actors and the shock of the guests in the inn.

'For a while, captain, it will seem to both you and others that you are still alive, that nothing has happened, until you experience your last love, until a woman with whom you could have offspring falls in love with you. Then, that very instant, you will vanish from the face of the earth, because the third soul cannot have offspring, just as someone who is vampired a third time cannot have children . . .'

Suddenly, from the floor above came the sound of the clarinet. This time someone was playing Haydn's *St Anthony's Chorale*. Upon hearing the sound, the captain leaped up as if scalded, stopped the show, quickly dismissed the actors and ran up to the cobble-stoned balcony.

A minute later, he stepped into the dining hall with a lady on his arm, who was carrying a blue pillow. Her deep cleavage was edged with perfumed artificial beauty marks, and she painted her little ear-holes red. On the captain's other arm was a young man with beautiful wavy hair, dressed in the uniform of an Austrian Hussar.

When she saw them with the captain, Dunja screamed into her sleeve, and the bells on the pillow of the captain's new guest tinkled. Then they heard Captain Opujić suddenly say, in a changed voice, as if chanting in church:

> *Enormous spaces did I cross, my Protectress,*
> > *in my worries,*
> *And nowhere refuge did I find,*
> > *or cover acquire.*
> *It is difficult to be alone, alone*
> > *among your Serbs*
> *A singing ring have I brought you,*
> > *but your eyes see me not from their veil.*

143

> *Youth shines not for your poet*
> *even at advanced age*
> *Your terrible dream calls me*
> *from mine*
> *And here, I see my heart rising*
> *in the gnawing night*
> *And setting to the sound*
> *of barbarian prayers.*

Following these words the captain introduced the newcomers as Mrs Rastina Kaloperović of Sremski Karlovci and her son Arsenije, second lieutenant in the Austrian army, who through a fortuitous combination of chance and circumstance were now, for the first time in a long time, meeting their daughter and sister respectively, the here present Dunja Kaloperović. Dunja rose and walked toward the newcomers, kissed her mother's bell-fringed blue pillow and her brother's mouth, and they all sat down.

'I can't recognize you. It's as if I'm seeing you for the first time. You've grown prettier since becoming my half-sister,' said Arsenije to Dunja. 'I've brought you something. Your earrings. Do you want to put them on?'

'Not here. Ears lose their virginity every time they are pierced with earrings; there's always a little blood,' smiled Dunja.

To Second Lieutenant Arsenije that smile seemed like an unfamiliar, expensive instrument which she played with peerless skill. Dunja looked her half-brother in the eyes and kissed the black spoon on her plate as if she were kissing him.

He's already noticed my feet, thought Jerisena

Tenecki angrily, eating mussels at the other end of the table, and she stared at Captain Opujić in astonishment. 'Is that the man who killed my father?'

As if hearing the question, Opujić the elder picked up his glass and rose to his feet to make a toast.

'*Mesdames*, you must be wondering whether the soul of a man such as the one standing before you right now is not steeped in soot. *Permettez-moi l'opportunité de vous expliquer mon cas* . . . I have chanted a lifetime's worth of church songs and stopped chanting. I have drunk two lifetime's worth of wine and pulled up both of my vineyards. I have strummed my fill of the *gusle* fiddle and broken it into pieces. Now I can say all I want to say . . . As you know, your fair sex often asks celebrated military leaders in this war for a lock of hair to remember them by. Admittedly, there are those of us here who have fared differently; we sometimes carry a lock of female hair on our wounded bodies as a sign that women healed us. Hidden in this male and female lock of hair is the difference between us soldiers and those who rule us. For people are divided into those who kill and those who hate. We soldiers, we are that ungifted breed that kills, plain riff-raff compared to the gifted power-holders who know how to hate. You can teach a man to use a sabre faster than a fork. But it takes generations to teach hate. It is a gift. Like a beautiful voice. A gift more dangerous than any sabre. If I had it I would not be a soldier, I would be making bells on the other side of the heavenly Danube in your Zemun, Mademoiselle Tenecki, I would drink wine from the most beautiful bell, a willow would grow out of one of my ears and grapes out of the other and I would not give a hoot about the iron cock on the roof of your foundry. I would sit happily in my rowing boat, catching wise fish and hating someone so much that somewhere in Paris their ears would drop off. But I lack the gift of hatred and so I must kill my enemies. However, those are sad tales, and this is a joyous day. After so many years I am reunited with my family again, and I want to drink this glass in that name and to the health of my loved ones. Vivat!'

Captain Opujić drank down his glass and hurled it through the window straight into the river. It fell among the walnut shells drifting along the mainstream in the dark.

In the morning the other bank of the river emerged from the mist, bathed in sunlight. It was high, eroded at the bottom and covered on top with grass which towered over the water like a long still wave under green foam. When the caravan set off, the young Opujić rode his filly almost naked, which was how he preferred to ride ever since removing his sabre, and caught up with his father, whom he asked whether the dinner bill had been settled, to which he received an answer.

'They charged each of us a Tuesday in April, and we took an hour's change! . . . I thought you were going to ask me when we Greeks and Serbs will save ourselves from misfortune, but all you want to know is about dinner.'

'So when will we save ourselves from misfortune?'

'When all Serb coffins are transformed into boats and when every such boat is tied to every plum tree in Servia.'

As the caravan travelled to the East through Greece,

with Mount Athos and the surrounding sea on its right, it was being whispered that the French consul was ill, that with each generation the men in his family died one year sooner and that this figure had already dropped to twenty-nine years of age.

'Try to look at the sun – you will see that it is like a copper shield with a black hole in the middle,' said Captain Opujić to his son, prodding the young man's boot with his own while riding along on his horse. The young Opujić cast him a fearful look, but his father raised his hand calmly and pointed into the distance.

'That is Constantinople! Waiting for you there in Fanar is Father Chrisostom with my gold coin in his mantle. I gave him and his shrine a present to marry you to Miss Tenecki. May it bring you luck!'

JUDGEMENT

THINK of Constantinople in Athens and that is one Constantinople, think of it in Rome and that is another.

It was early autumn when they came to rest in the huge town built on three seas and behind four winds, on two stretches of land and under the green glass of the Bosphorus. The nights rolled up like socks in their house above the water, a house that counted the boats and winds as the two of them went down to the shore to purchase fragrant oils. Jerisena adored doing that, and whenever the opportunity arose they would stop by the little shop in the middle of Misir Bazaar, facing the Golden Horn, to drink white tea with hashish and watch the children fish without bait. The fish were so plentiful there that the children simply tossed in empty hooks and pulled out their catch. There in that shop they met a strange little man with a cord on his shirt in place of a collar; he, they were told, was of Serb blood but Turkish faith. Once a month the man would come down to the Golden Horn through the Kapali Market and stop by the shop to buy fragrances. His conversation with the shopkeeper was always the same, as if the two of them were repeating some sort of prayer.

'He used to be a mason,' the shopkeeper told them, 'but now he suffers from a strange sickness; time passes much faster in his sleep than in his waking hours, and every night he lives through at least a decade, so that here in Constantinople even the oldest of people do not know his age. He may not know it himself.'

The afternoon that they saw him in the shop he had come in looking transfixed and asked to buy anything.

'Sandalwood?' asked the fragrance merchant as he slipped a small opaque glass vial under a larger bottle and waited. They waited together in the semi-darkness, but nothing happened. And then, just as the customer was about to give up and leave, the merchant said, 'It takes as long as it does to read a sura of the Koran.'

As the customer was illiterate, he did not know how long it took to read a sura of the Koran; finally, appearing from the lip of the upended larger bottle was something like a comet, gleaming like a drop, and it slowly slid down its tail and into the smaller vial.

'Do you want to try?' asked the merchant, wiping the rim of the bottle's neck neatly with his finger and offering it to the customer. The latter took a little from the finger on to his own and then moved to wipe it on his robe.

'No, not on your robe!' the merchant cautioned. 'It will burn. On the palm of your hand. First on the palm of your hand.' And when the customer complied and wanted to smell it, the merchant stopped him.

'No, not today, sir, not today! In three days' time! That is when the real fragrance will appear. And it will last as long as sweat. But it will be stronger than sweat, because it has the strength of a tear . . .'

This was the conversation Sofronije and Jerisena overheard by the Golden Horn that day, and the merchant invited them to come back for tea again; he had something special to offer them.

'The day is for love and the night is for song,' they were told by Father Chrisostom, whom they visited in his little church in Fanar. 'Because love sees, and night hears.'

As they listened to these words, from the sea on the fresco in the semi-darkness behind them appeared fish and monsters disgorging men, women and children with musical instruments in their hands, their music and hymns responding to the sound of the angels' trumpets, calling them to Judgement Day.

They married on the Sunday of the Holy Trinity, at a moment when they loved each other more than ever before.

Jerisena Opujić often took her husband to the Temple of Wisdom, which under the Turks was no longer a church but was not a mosque either. They entered the immense, heavy shadow of the church which was to the temple what death is to sleep. Waiting there inside the church was a tall pillar with a bronze shield nailed to the stone. The shield had a

hole into which you put your thumb, traced a circle
with the rest of your hand and made a wish. But God
rewards those he loves with the greatest fortune and
the greatest misfortune at once. Which was why
Sofronije did not dare go in. Sitting in the shadow of
the huge edifice, he felt that the temple had another
shadow as well. Down below, under its foundations, in
the womb of the earth, domes, choirs and stairways
revealed themselves, along with slanting plinths of
stone which led deep down to the salty subterranean
waters of the Bosphorus and the fresh waters of the
land, reflecting the temple above, like an echo imitat-
ing the word. This subterranean outline was com-
posed of sounds but also of hard materials, just like
the one above it. Holy wisdom was reflected not only
in the water but in the earth as well.

Also reflected in the earth was the sky above it.
Suddenly, there in the shadow of Holy Sophia,
Sofronije started to follow the movements of the constellations of metals underground, which, like echo
and sound, were unerringly connected with the constellation of stars in the sky, and under the crust of the
earth he clearly distinguished the movements of
Cancer, Libra, Leo and Virgo. He was becoming an
astrologer of the Zodiac's underground belt. But he
felt that his craving, or hunger, which drove him to all
this, was merely an apprenticeship in preparation for
complete satiation and the perennial gratification of
desire. And he did not dare enter the temple.

Your thought is a candle and with it you can light
someone else's candle, for which you need fire,
thought Sofronije. But his fire was still under the
earth.

And so it continued until one day the merchant invited them to tea again. He had acquired the thing he had long since wanted to show them. When they went down into his shop, they found there the little man with the cord around his neck. He smelt of ebony and the merchant whispered to them that that was the smell of the old man's sweat.

'His ears sweat. But his sweat is at least a century-and-a-half old,' added the merchant, smiling as he removed a coin from his turban and showed it to them in the palm of his hand.

'Money minted in hell,' he whispered, and the coin began to glitter as if in response to his words. Taking a bucket of water from under the counter and placing it in front of them, the merchant asked Jerisena to toss the coin into the water. The coin refused to sink. Jerisena was amazed, but Sofronije, carrying the shadow of Holy Wisdom inside him, sensed that the coin was minted from a mixture of copper, silver and glass, even though this was the first time he had ever seen it. Indeed, when he put the coin in his mouth, he heard inside it the humming of silver ore and the chime of glass made in the subterranean fire. And rising above this hum was something that sounded like a copper trumpet.

'There are two more coins like that one,' said the mason, who had been following the whole thing.

'That one can buy your tomorrow, the other can buy your today and yesterday,' he told Sofronije, and Jerisena had the feeling that this was not the first time the mason and Sofronije had met, that they knew each other from before, that they had something like an arrangement to meet right here, in Misir Bazaar.

As if corroborating her thoughts, without a word the young Opujić paid for his coin. And the next day he went straight to Holy Sophia.

As soon as he entered the temple he felt lost in the immense square which in fact was the domed church. Everything inside was shrouded in darkness, broken only by the light of the sun streaking in through the huge keyholes. He ran his eye over all the pillars in the temple but saw no copper plate. The only thing that glittered on one of the pillars was a ray of sun at eye-level. Stepping closer, he discovered under this shaft of light the shield with its hole. He slid his thumb inside as if it were the hole of a huge copper trumpet and traced a circle around it with his hand, murmuring his sworn desire. Nothing happened.

Sofronije Opujić never expected matters concerning him suddenly to change so much that it would be immediately noticeable. But he did find it strange that he felt nothing. When he got home, he told Jerisena that the thing had been done. She embraced him, stepped over to the window and spat the pebble containing his secret into the Bosphorus.

'No more secrets, no more concealing! Everything will now come true. Was it like waking up?'

She behaved as if it was a holiday, she brought out candied flowers, roses and jasmine in sweet oil, they sat on the huge window, which was in fact the cannon port on their house, and remembered *The Thousand and One Arabian Nights* and their calculations.

'Perhaps we don't have children because we haven't worked out which was the night Scheherazade got pregnant and what was the story she told that night,' said Jerisena, looking at her own Sofronije Opujić and feeling that love had aged him.

'There are truths man helps to die,' she said. 'Man himself is a truth that dies. Mankind is always seventeen years old, but I no longer am!'

That night she heard Sofronije pulling himself free of the huge dog-hair blanket he was wrapped in. She heard the stubble of his beard tear the pillow and saw the navel-like dimple on his chin and was surprised. In the morning she told him:

'Every great love is a kind of punishment.'

'You know, all of us have a contract with God. Half of everything we have or do, half of time, strength or beauty, half of our dealings and travels are left to us, the other half goes to God. And it is the same with love. Half of our love is left to us, the other half goes to its Maker, and there it remains in a more beautiful place, lasting for ever, no matter what happens to our half of love here. Think of it as something beautiful and joyous!'

But it was all in vain. Her body no longer smelt of peaches when he was near her or touched her, Jerisena no longer painted her breasts the same colour as her lips. She looked at her husband without understanding what he was telling her. As for him, just as he had once approached Jerisena at tremendous speed, so now he suddenly began to move away from her at terrible speed, like a constellation. Just as he had been unable to resist the inexorable attraction, so now he could do nothing against this dizzying, irrevocable retreat.

Jerisena then said to him, 'You were right! Great love makes one stupid. And we have become stupid. At least I have. And I can't fly any more. Not even in my dreams, let alone in the room. Perhaps love can kill'

And she thought: Perhaps with another man I could have a child.

$\mathcal{T}$HE $\mathcal{W}$ORLD

$\mathcal{S}$OON after arriving in Constantinople in 1813 the French envoy decided to throw a garden party at his residence. The guests were entertained by fortune-tellers and dancers, and the music was already playing when people began strolling into the boy-envoy's spacious house. The captain brought Dunja, who looked as if she had been crying all night. Mrs Rastina Kaloperović, wearing silver powder in her hair, came with her son, and the young Kaloperović, scanning the large room for someone, was surprised to see an oval window on the wall facing the next room. It had a frame in the shape of a gilded wreath, which made the window look like a painting. It reminded Sofronije of a window in his parents' drawing-room in Trieste.

In the garden outside, the captain's cavalrymen had started up a round dance, and the lead dancer so shortened his step that it was difficult to know where his heels began and toes ended.

Jerisena whispered, 'The round dance is a labyrinth.'

The guests were still assembling, their host was sporting a pigeon-blue tunic without insignia, blue silk hair and, as always, a belt of silk around his waist. His secretary was attired in black, with silver clasps on his clothes and belt. The worry on his face suited him as much as the lack of it suited the boy in blue standing next to him, although it was present in the boy's boots, which kept looking for their place. Suddenly the room went dark and in the picture/window a nude appeared like a living picture, with a veil draped across its thighs. It was difficult to tell its sex, although its chest was bare. To women the chest looked like a man's, to men it looked like a little girl's. When the dance was over, the apparition struck the pose of a living picture in its frame. It stood with one leg bent at the knee and somewhere this reminded the young Opujić of his own body's position when he was hung from the tree on the orders of Captain Tenecki. Except this apparition was standing, not hanging.

Suddenly a dozen gypsy girls burst into the house and garden, the bells on their skirt hems jingling, and they began to read the guests' fortunes from the cards.

The captain cried out, 'Tarocchi! Tarocchi!' He grabbed his son by the hand and planted him in the garden next to a fortune-teller.

'Cards, sir, are like a language. But take heed now. Do you want a big secret or a small one? And whose fortune do you want me to tell?'

'Both of ours from the same cards,' said the captain.

'A big secret,' said Sofronije.

'All right, sir. Do not laugh while I read the cards
because it will do you harm. Each of you must ask a
question, but to yourselves so that I don't hear it.'

The woman spread open a scarf in front of her,
remarking, 'It's not good to do it on a rock', took
twenty-two cards out of a leather pouch and handed
them to the Opujićes to 'warm'. When the cards were
shuffled, Sofronije cut them and Haralampije made
the sign of the cross over them. With her left hand the
gypsy lay the cards out like a cross on the scarf, and in
the middle she placed one card horizontally across a
vertical card. Turning them over, she said to the
young Opujić, 'Your father was killed. And you are
hiding a big secret.'

'My father was not killed,' laughed the young
Opujić. Whereupon the fortune-teller looked aghast
at Captain Opujić, scooped up her cards and fled
from the house just as the guests were being called to
dinner.

With their last morsels of food and encroaching
fatigue, the French envoy's guests listened to the
music. Second Lieutenant Kaloperović was staring
fixedly at his half-sister Dunja as if bewitched, when
suddenly his mother, upon seeing that look, said, 'I
hope you remember our pledge. Have you carried
out your part of the pledge? Have you bedded her?'

'Who, Dunja? Yes. Back in the inn already.'

Madam Rastinja laughed bitterly.

'By my count,' she said into her son's ear, 'there is only a bit left to fulfil our pledge. I still have two steps left, and you have one.'

'One?' said the young Kaloperović anxiously, but his mother stroked him with her silvery eyes.

'The last one,' she observed offhandedly, 'will be our joint step.'

Just then somebody started softly singing 'Memories Are the Sweat of the Soul' in Greek, but it was the same song that Sofronije and Jerisena loved as their own.

And then Sofronije took the most decisive step of his life. Moved by the singing, he tried to catch the eye of his wife, sitting beside him. But he failed. Jerisena was listening to the song, gazing straight ahead of her, breathing heavily. Then she raised her eyes. Combing her hair absentmindedly with her fingers, her gaze was directed at the dark window of a neighbouring building, behind which stood a wall cloaked in darkness, and behind that wall reigned the vast night full of water and grass. And so her gaze first hit upon the window, then reached the wall cloaked in darkness and then moved still further on, although Jerisena no longer saw anything there. Her gaze followed a straight path to the East through the woods, it glided over the Black Sea, travelled through Odessa, across the steppes, missed some Caspian fishermen on a night trawl, passed through the Caucasus mountains, through Pamir and for a moment waned at the Great Wall of China, not because of fatigue or because this was too big an obstacle for her gaze to handle but because Jerisena did not see what she was yearning to see and so had simply stopped looking in that direction. And then, shivering from the song she was listening to, Jerisena's eyes finally found Captain Haralampije Opujić, her husband's father, at the next table, and her whole body began to smell of peaches.

Horrified, Sofronije looked at Jerisena, while Jerisena looked rapturously at his father. They sat motionless like that for a few seconds and then Sofronije noticed that Jerisena was painting her breasts and lips the same colour again and that the little silver shoe was no longer hanging around her neck. Jerisena had removed the third shoe.

She will have with my father the child she could not have with me, it occurred to him.

And at that moment the hunger that for years had been growing under Sofronije Opujić's heart like a small pain faded and turned into a great pain. Everything that had ever hurt him began to hurt him again. All the old wounds on his body and soul stirred to life, all his childhood scars were aroused and started up again, and the lock of dark hair and lock of red dropped off his body. After seventeen years his sex organ collapsed, his right boot stopped pinching him, his listening power was cut short and he stopped hearing underground. And the whole wide world opened up before him. Horrified, he wanted to pull back, to wrench off his thumb, but it was too late. Somewhere far away from him his sworn desire was coming true in the best possible way, working for him regardless of, perhaps even in spite of, him but at a devastating price. Someone omnipotent was fulfilling his wish but depriving him of Jerisena's love. Somewhere, who knows where (Sofronije feared), signs of mercy were already coming, travelling like whirlwinds, and he felt an easing of his soul, he felt that things both around and inside him were shifting, that the decision had been taken, making future decisions easier for him. He heard the constellations rename themselves in his favour and his own sign of the Zodiac change from Libra to Scorpio, and that changed the taste of venison with mushrooms in his mouth. Everything that existed, that was, that he knew, suddenly became unfamiliar and strange; and everything that was not, that did not exist, became clear and familiar. As if every card of his destiny, his entire Major Arcana, had been laid down reversed, Sofronije's life was turned upside down, his senses inverted and redirected from the underground to the cosmos.

God rewards his favourites with the greatest fortune and the greatest misfortune at the same time, he thought, and was about to cry when suddenly he heard his father chatting away at the table:

'Even smiles need to be translated, my dear lady, as if they were words! A French smile, for instance, is difficult to translate into Greek. A Jewish smile is untranslatable, and Germans will not laugh unless there is a price-tag on the joke . . .'

While the captain was chatting, while Sofronije Opujić was sitting and looking at his wife, and she at his father, someone was looking at Sofronije. Mrs Rastina Kaloperović, holding the belled pillow in her arms, was devouring him with her eyes. For Sofronije was her daughter Dunja's penultimate lover with whom she had not yet slept. He was the penultimate step of her pledge, which would then be fulfilled and crowned with a joint last step. Hers and Arsenije's. In brief, Sofronije Opujić was the only obstacle still standing between Madam Rastina and the bed of her son Arsenije Kaloperović.

Mrs Kaloperović's gaze was momentarily interrupted by Captain Opujić, who tapped his knife against his glass and rose to toast the French emperor. And then something unimaginable happened.

In front of everyone in the garden of the French envoy in Constantinople, Captain Haralampije Opujić vanished without a trace, along with his glass. The only thing the servants found under his chair the next morning was a pair of bloodstained spurs.

APPENDIX 1

WAYS TO LAY OUT
THE TAROT CARDS

THE MAGIC CROSS

The simplest layout in the Tarot, giving the order in which the cards are to be laid out and read.

THE CELTIC CROSS

Gives the order in which the cards are to be laid out and read. The fifth card represents the fate of the Querent (whose fortune is being read), the four cards in front represent the past, and those behind represent the future. The tenth card represents the advice of the fortune-teller.

165

The Great Triad

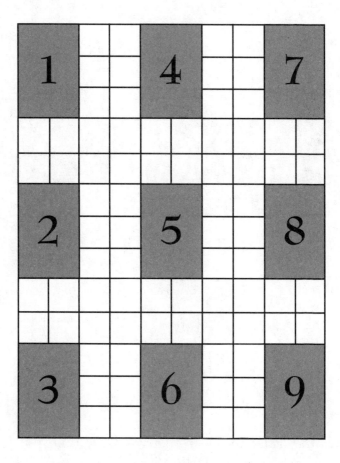

Gives the order in which the cards are to be laid out and read. The first three cards refer to the past, the next three to the present and the last three to the future of the Querent.

The Keys of the Great Secret for Ladies of Both Sexes

Special Key *The Fool*
Right side up: Fickleness but with a happy outcome. A choice is offered. Paths, new experiences.
Reversed (upside down): Foul play. Beware of head blows. Displays of hatred in environment.

The First Seven Keys

Key 1 *The Magician*
Right side up: Salutary knowledge, creative energy. Originality. Good moment for business. Personality of the male Querent.
Reversed: Decline, charlatanism, bad beginning.

Key 2 *The Papess*
Right side up: Pure luck, hidden influences. The card denotes harmony and the mother of knowledge, the teacher of understanding. The personality of the female Querent.
Reversed: Inconstancy, unfaithfulness in marriage, misjudgements.

Key 3 *The Empress*
Right side up: Fertility, femininity, material wealth, inheritance of real estate.
Reversed: Rash behaviour, slump in business. Lost illusions. Exhaustion.

Key 4 *The Emperor*
Right side up: Protection, leadership. Help or wise advice in overcoming crises. Well-meaning energy.
Reversed: Cruel and arrogant power-wielder. Monetary crisis, ineptitude, bad advice. Whatever is done will be no good.

Key 5 *The Heirophant*
Right side up: Conduct based on convention. Selfless partner in love affair. Excellent decision. Adaptability. Wisdom, broad prospects.
Reversed: Intolerance. Underhandedness. Non-achievement. Enormous difficulties in the offing. Miscalculation in business, brief love affairs.

Key 6 *The Lovers*
Right side up: Hesitation, choosing between two loves. Health.
Reversed: Unrequited love. Neurotic amorous strivings. Love ceases, relationship based on self-interest.

Key 7 *The Chariot*
Right side up: Success. Triumph of the mind over convention.
Reversed: Unexpected failure. Listlessness and illness.

The Second Seven Keys

Key 8 *Strength*
Right side up: Triumph of love over hate. Sincerity. Security, physical and spiritual energy.
Reversed: Anger. Obstruction from the immediate environment, conflicts, great difficulties.

Key 9 *The Hermit*
Right side up: Wisdom is offered. Prudence. Good decisions. Experience. Healer.
Reversed: Solitude, sorrow. Useless advice.

Key 10 *The Wheel of Fortune*
Right side up: Change, rise and fall, good luck. Earnings.
Reversed: Belated plans, indecision.

Key 11 *Justice*
Right side up: Balance, karma, legal matters. Judge.
Reversed: Law suit. Injustice from unexpected quarters.

Key 12 *The Hanged Man*
Right side up: Atonement, sacrifice. Intuition. Self-consolidation in realms of higher wisdom. The passage between earthly and spiritual interests. Events we cannot influence but which do not necessarily turn out badly.
Reversed: Disorientation, separation. Wasted effort. Re-examination of one's own actions.

Key 13 *Death*
Right side up: Transformation, change, renewal. Gains.
Reversed: Struggle, illness, melancholy. Sudden impoverishment or change for the worse. Mourning.

Key 14 *Temperance*
Right side up: Patience, harmonization, mental peace, but also a warning.
Reversed: Love without harmony. Indolence. Actions which lead to regret. Recent decision bears bitter fruits.

The Third Seven Keys

Key 15 *The Devil*
Right side up: Fatality, three demons, materialism. Magnetism, supernatural abilities. Bad company.
Reversed: Venereal disease, danger, unwanted pregnancy.

Key 16 *The Tower*
Right side up: Catastrophe, destruction, discarding of selfish ambitions and previous way of life.
Reversed: Unpredictability, enemies, chaos. Ill health.

Key 17 *The Star*
Right side up: Hope, health, inspiration. Wishes fulfilled, creativity.
Reversed: Unfavourable position, dampened spirits. Disappointment in loved ones.

Key 18 *The Moon*
Right side up: Deception, unforeseen perils. Hypocrisy, envy from others. Infidelity. Pregnancy. Intuition, dreams, imagination at work.
Reversed: Illusions, hidden dangers, mental illness, unfertile imagination.

Key 19 *The Sun*
Right side up: Happiness, liberation, marriage. Health.
Reversed: Vanity, misunderstandings. Minor ailments.

Key 20 *Judgement*

Right side up: Spiritual awakening, adaptation. Transcending the earthly. Protection. A seemingly unsolvable matter is resolved.
Reversed: Unconscientious, rash decision. A long-standing love affair is ended.

Key 21 *The World*

Right side up: Joy, success in all undertakings, reward, wishes fulfilled. Beginning of long-term happiness.
Reversed: This is Hermes' card ('Above as Below'),and reads the same reversed as right side up. It is already the twelfth card reversed: The Hanged Man.

Ways to Lay Out the Tarot Cards

The Magic Cross
The Great Triad
The Celtic Cross

The Fool

The Magician

The Papess

The Empress

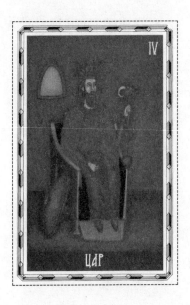

The Emperor

The Heirophant

The Lovers

The Chariot

175

Strength

The Hermit

The Wheel of Fortune

Justice

The Hanged Man

Death

Temperance

The Devil

180

The Tower

The Star

The Moon

The Sun

Judgement   The World

184